COFFIN IN OXFORD

GWENDOLINE BUTLER

Praise For Gwendoline Butler

'Gwendoline Butler is excellent on the bizarre fantasies of other people's lives and on modern paranoia overlaying old secrets; and her plots have the rare ability to shock'
ANDREW TAYLOR, THE INDEPENDENT

'[Butler's] inventiveness never seems to flag; and the singular atmosphere of her books, compounded of jauntiness and menace, remains undiminished'
PATRICIA CRAIG, TLS

'Butler distils her own brand of disquiet: omnipresent and irresistible'
JOHN COLEMAN, THE SUNDAY TIMES

'The imaginary Second City of London... together with its well drawn characters, make this a quietly compelling read'
JOHN WELCOME, THE IRISH INDEPENDENT

Gwendoline Butler

COFFIN IN OXFORD

CT

First published in Great Britain by Geoffrey Bles 1962
This edition 1998 CT Publishing.
Copyright © Gwendoline Butler 1962

A CIP catalogue record for this book is available from the
British Library.

ISBN 1 902002 00 8

9 8 7 6 5 4 3 2 1

Book design and Typography by Crow Media Design.
Printed and bound in Great Britain by Cox & Wyman Ltd,
Reading, Berks.

For the amusement of
Nancy Waterston

COFFIN IN OXFORD

Dramatis Personae

INSPECTOR JOHN COFFIN, from London

JOANNA DUFFY

TED ROMAN

EUGENE CZARNKOWSKI

FRANCESCA ROSE ARMOUR

MISS MARTIN BROWN

SIR JOE AND LADY DUFFY

LORD CHARLETON

MR SHARDLOES

REVD. FATHER MAHONEY

INSPECTOR PETER PINCHING, of Oxford

GWENDOLINE BUTLER

Chapter 1

The First Triangle

THERE ARE A HUNDRED BELLS to listen to in Oxford: the great bell of Christ Church, the bells of Magdalen, the light voiced bell of Keble, the feminine bell of Lady Margaret Hall. And all of them were bells that Gene detested.

Oxford as Gene saw it was just another place to live; he would have preferred New York but since the USA wasn't ready to have him just yet he made do with Oxford. Like a cat, with four paws and all of them firmly on the ground, he knew how to make himself comfortable. He was a keen little cat.

Eugene Stanislas Czarnkowski was certainly his name (or one of his names) or had been his name, for he was always known as Gene and he assured them that his full name was too long, too foreign and too obscure for anyone ever to remember. It was certainly known somehow in the Home Office files, for they had him down

11

GWENDOLINE BUTLER

there as a legitimate and permitted refugee although so far they had not accepted him as a British subject. Every so often Gene applied and every so often was obscurely refused. He said he was waiting for someone in the Home Office to die and when they went he would get his citizenship. If he didn't die himself first. After each refusal he was a little low but soon cheered up again and resumed life on his normal terms.

Even normal life was not too placid for Gene. He was always involved, he always took an interest, he had *feelings*. Detachment meant nothing to Gene; he was the complete partisan. It was perhaps his most loveable quality. To English people another endearing characteristic was that he loved animals. He had a wry, ironic affection for children, pretending to regard them as frightening little creatures, and that didn't go down too badly either in Oxford, where the children, big and little, can be formidable indeed. With all this *angst*, there was yet a deep-down streak of worldliness in Gene that showed itself in a placid enjoyment of good food, well-polished furniture, and the efficient running of his small business.

Everyone ought to have a Gene in their lives to add flavour and sometimes even alarms, for there was no doubt with Gene you rocked from crisis to crisis, always something impending but never quite turning up. He was going to be involved in disaster tomorrow, next week, or the day after that, but somehow when that time came round there he was pretty much as usual and *that* crisis, whether of work or love or spies, forgotten. After tottering on the edge of volcanoes for so long with Gene you got to think he always cried wolf. This was how Joanna and everyone felt when he started worrying about Ted. But this time, about Ted, he wasn't crying wolf, or if he was it was in answer to a deep-down animal call.

Ted was brought round from the first attack, if you could call it an attack, with difficulty. He had been found shut up in a narrow cupboard with a scarf tightened round his neck: his own scarf, to add insult to injury. And instead of sympathy and alarm, all he got was long looks and a quiet word from his doctor to go to a psychiatrist. While Ted, bewildered, puzzled, innocent (or very nearly), guileless, who had been expecting sympathy and had never heard of the psychology of agoraphobia, didn't know what they were getting at.

The second attack was similar, but milder. He was simply discovered with his tie round his neck throttling him.

Gene knew all about these attacks.

Ted very nearly lost his job as a result. He didn't quite, though afterwards he bitterly regretted it. It was thought that Ted had, after all, had the sense not to do it at school so that this last step

13

need not be taken. The Slade School of Art after its wartime sojourn in Oxford had left a tiny offshoot of itself in the city in St. Ebbe's by the river and Christ Church, and this was where Ted taught. He had daily classes and also evening classes and his pupils were a mixed bag. As well as youngsters fresh from school he had housewives, and one railwayman. Ted was proud of them all, and they were proud of him, he wasn't one of those artists who loathed the business of teaching. He thought it gave him as much as it took. "But you've got vitality for six," one of the older teachers used to say. Ted was tall and fair haired and with a pleasant look to him even if he was not good looking. He did have to shift his digs, though; but in his restless, shiftless career he had done this often. But he *had* thought he was rooted this time. He looked round his little room sadly as he packed. That scar on the wall represented the time the boys came in for a beer and threw a bottle at the wall, that coffee stain on the door mat stood for the excitement when he sold his first big picture (got his first big write-up) and dropped his breakfast cup in excitement, and that smear of lipstick on the wall by the mirror was Joanna. Joanna. He stroked the smear lovingly. "Goodbye Joanna, even that little bit of you."

"You do see, Ted darling," pleaded his landlady, "with all these girls in the house, I can't."

Ted nodded.

"Heaven knows I respect you as an artist, Ted," she said helplessly. Francesca often looked helpless but she wasn't for all that. She ran a lodging house for research students. You had to be tough to do that. And she had two boys of her own and one girl, now decorating various expensive schools, and you didn't do *that* on being helpless. There was something about Francesca that suggested she herself did not always know the limits of her own character. "As an artist," she repeated.

For Ted was a fine artist, possibly even a great one, and very soon now, if he *survived*, the critics would acknowledge this. 'It's a shame', thought Francesca Armour, 'that he can't be packed off to a farm or something'. (Francesca always thought of a farm or the country as the place where you worked off trouble.) But the necessity of earning a living rooted Ted in Oxford. 'Heaven knows I've nothing against artists being neurotic; it may even be necessary for them. If only he could have lived in Paris in the time of Toulouse Lautrec. Anything would be forgiven a man with his eye for mass and colour.' She signed her name carefully to his receipted bill. Francesca always signed everything as if she were curiously anxious to establish her name and personality. Francesca Rose Armour, she wrote. Rose. "I always feel my second name belongs to another person," she used to say. "I'd *be* another person

15

if I ever used it."

"Keep in touch, Ted," she said.

"Oh don't worry," said Ted gruffly. "I'll go it alone. It's the colonial in me." For Ted, as well as being an artist and very young, was an Australian. A New Australian. His mother had been killed during the War. His father had disappeared, never to be seen again. Or that was the story.

So that summer Ted moved from lodging to lodging, never quite able to settle, and eventually into his little studio down in St. Ebbe's.

On one of his moves he took with him an unlocked trunk.

But because he was anxious and perturbed he told his trouble to the member of his art class that he trusted most, the old railwayman.

And *he* told his sister.

His sister had a friend, a nurse, and they discussed it kindly enough together and the nurse told her friend in London, Mrs. Coffin. She was mother to John Coffin, London policeman. She did not immediately tell her son, but carried the story round in her mind, and it was there ready to be tapped when needed.

So by a remote chain of events John Coffin was contacted. It was odd, but, as John Coffin said, many things in police life are. A genuine, real coincidence.

Joanna did as much as she could to help Ted in his moves through those weeks of summer. She knew how difficult it was to find the right place to live although she herself had a pretty tiny flat on the top of the house in Park Town perched high in Victorian Gothic. She knew the rumours and startling gossip that Ted's 'accidents' (everyone put them in quotation marks) had brought into being. But she didn't believe them. She just didn't believe them. Ted was not like that. She never discussed it with Ted, although as a doctor she would have been capable of clinical detachment. She doubted if Ted would, though; there was nothing clinically detached about him.

But she clung to the belief that he was basically straightforward and healthy. Because she thought he loved her. And no one wants to be loved by a pervert, by someone who is crooked inside. Nor did she talk to Francesca Armour about it, although Francesca was a good friend, because Francesca had shown her hand when she asked Ted to leave. Francesca was a little hipped about sex since her husband died and was not a fair judge. She was wanting to think badly about the male sex. In any case Francesca was away from home these summer months.

There were others, of course, in Joanna's world whom she could consult. There was Gene. Her friends and her relations, they were all the same really. Oxford to Joanna was a *little* world. It ended at Park Town where she lived on the north, and at Folly Bridge on the south. Three or four square miles and in it all the learning and scholarship that counted. It was a charming insularity and it would have shocked Joanna to know she displayed it. But it seemed a disloyalty to Ted to talk about him, so she occupied herself in shopping for him and occasionally cooking him a square meal. She was busy herself that summer working as a paediatrician and pathologist in a big Oxford hospital. She was writing a thesis. "Absolutely essential in my trade," she used to say, "to write a thesis if you want to get ahead." This was her cynical public attitude but underneath she cared frightfully about the subject of her thesis which was:

A Study of the Origins and Development of a B^1 Virus Infection in the cases of twenty newly-born Infants.

She minded that those babies died. She wanted to save them. It was probably going to be a very bad thesis. She knew you shouldn't care, that it should be the patient piling-up of fact upon fact that was your pleasure and your pain, and that generalisations and *results*, especially results that could be acted upon, should come like grace from heaven, unwished and unasked for. To know where you wanted to go was, academically speaking, in a thesis, death.

Charming, learned, unworldly, loving Joanna waited upon her fate.

18

Her fate, glowering, moved into his studio. Ted was out of humour. He hoped this was positively his last move. He lovingly unpacked his paints, brushes, technical equipment, and arranged them in a place of honour. Then he dragged his clothes, two pairs of terylene trousers, clean and grubby, best and workers, three sweaters and seventeen shirts, into a corner. He was home.

He pushed the big dark brown trunk into the corner of the room and put a blanket on the top. He didn't try to conceal it in any way. It wasn't locked.

It was the last week of July, and he had before him, he thought, the whole of August and something of September to devote to his own work. And he knew what this work was to be. Ted set to work with grim determination to prepare his canvas and his palette. He was pre-eminently a technician and a craftsman. It was typical of him that he underpainted a good deal with pink fleshy tones which gave a thick, living glow to his canvas.

There can be nothing more satisfying to the artist than to know what his big piece of work is to be, to see it before him in the full beauty of its subject before reality has shortened and dulled it, and when there is time and opportunity to do it. Ted had this satisfaction and because of it, although he was deeply disturbed inside, he could not be truly unhappy.

Ted knew that now was the time to paint Gene.

Gene, a Polish émigré and possibly a good many other things beside, had appeared in England in 1936, had been interned in the Isle of Man in 1940 (where he had been so happy that he had gone back for a holiday every year afterwards) and had come to Oxford towards the end of the war and set himself up in a typing agency. "For scholars," he said, "entirely for scholars." It was soon the sort of finicking female job that appealed to him.

Joanna and Ted were bound to Gene with ties of affection and loyalty. He had been the first person to really encourage Ted to develop his style of painting, to encourage him that there was not only an end but a *here* and *now*, a beginning to be made. And then he had introduced the pair to each other.

Joanna and Ted looked after him as well as they could. And he in his turn when Ted was ill and injured gave him a tender, even womanly care. "You'd make a splendid nurse," said Ted, woe-begone in his dressing gown, nursing his despised injury after the first incident.

Gene had settled straight away into an Oxford ready to receive him. It was an Oxford of retirement. There was the old General up the Woodstock Road, a Bishop, an ex-colonial Governor, an old Ambassador. Among these once booming, now partially silenced big guns, Gene fluted his own contrived little tune. The bond was that they were all writing their memoirs and he was getting them typed.

All the old gentlemen dined together on a Wednesday in every month at one or other of the colleges delighted to receive them (for they were all really famous old men). They characteristically understated this as 'The Evening', but enjoyed it with great gusto, bringing to it distinguished guests: the Chancellor of the Exchequer, a visiting diplomat, and even once a great, definitely non-gentleman jockey. An ex-queen, reputed to be the lover of Joanna's uncle, old Sir Joe, the diplomat, had appeared on one occasion.

Although it appeared so informal, an outsider stood as much chance of getting in as a butter-ball in Hell. The rules were all the more rigid for not being expressed. You had to have known all the members for the last fifty odd years. That was all; but that was enough. It restricted membership to one or two schools and even one or two professions.

The old Ambassador retained his distinction. He had been accustomed to service; it had left its traces in a certain nattiness in his arrangements; sherry was served on a silver tray, always two sorts of sherry. A tin of biscuits stood by his bed.

He had been used to being heard and this came out too. He knew the answers to everything: he knew that the Albanian economy depended upon apples: grow more apples and they would be rich: that Poland needed lumber mills, that all Poles were very like Irishmen, so that you could treat them in the same way. He knew all the answers but unluckily some of the questions were pretty dusty old ones by now and the answers were what nobody wanted.

He had represented his country honourably and was now retired with a knighthood. He lived in a small flat and did his own washing up. Joanna loved him.

"The Poles are just like the Irish," said the old Ambassador in delight. "Charming, ebullient, full of vitality. Great horsemen too."

"And wonderful with women," he said, slapping Joanna on the back.

"Gene doesn't even think of me in that way," she protested.

"No, but *you* ought to."

Gene was pre-eminently successful at an occupation usually reserved for women, but which gave Gene scope for all his skill with people, all his neat-fingered technical skill, all his expertise. Anxious scholars were gentled and soothed, they had faith that their much-amended manuscripts, with additions and subtractions flying about on bits of paper like flags would be delivered safely by their chosen obstetrician: a whole baby with all its legs and arms complete, and no tiresome little holes in its tummy.

Ted had made a rough charcoal sketch of the projected portrait. Gene had given him one short sitting. It had all Gene's force and originality. Gene was small-boned, neat and bright-eyed. He said he was forty but he could just as easily have been fifty or thirty with his sleek, pale hair and plump, gentle figure. One blemish was a puce scar down the side of his face. It was an old scar and Gene always said it resulted from an injury so old he no longer remembered its origin. He had been a baby.

Ted looked at the beginning of his picture of Gene and hummed quietly. It was good, it was going to be great. It was no more than a cartoon, a sketch for what he wanted to do, but it had the qualities he was hoping for. Paint would be better than charcoal. Gene was eminently paintable.

Gene was having a Bad Day, Joanna had observed with amusement. Good and Bad Days appeared capriciously in Gene's life and seemed to bear little resemblance to what actually took place. "Today is a Bad Day," or "a Good Day," Gene would proclaim and that was that. You knew a bad day by Gene's jokes, which were worse than ever, the little tunes he hummed and the strength of the coffee. On Bad Days it was very, very strong. Joanna found herself almost looking forward to the Bad Days.

She listened to Gene humming. "What's that?" she said absently

"From *The Marriage of Figaro*. It's sung to a little page-boy who is off to the Wars. Wars with a capital, mark you."

"Poor fellow."

"It's a girl-singer dressed up as a boy really." He hummed. "I love opera. My favourite is *Rosenkavalier*."

"Didn't someone once call it an opera about a girl dressed up as a boy pretending to be a girl?"

"Many operas are on that theme," said Gene. "And a great deal of Shakespeare."

"Which brings me," said Joanna, "to what I wanted to discuss."

Their eyes met. Gene knew what she meant. He sat down. "Ted?"

"Ted. Who started this scare that Ted was a super neurotic? Two funny accidents that could be just that and the whole thing blows up. Why?"

"There could be things about the accidents we do not know," said Gene carefully. "There is perhaps a background?"

Joanna looked at him. He was sitting turning over the pages of a typescript. She recognised it, from the corrections giving the effect of a palimpsest, as her paternal uncle's memoirs. She could see the words 'Marshal Schuizoyr, the

24

Chancellor, told me over the wine in his hunting lodge one night.'

"Are you asking me a question?" she said. "Or telling me?"

"I am telling you," said Gene. He got up and poured her out a cup of coffee, it was lukewarm and bitter black. "There will be a background. In my experience there is always a background."

"I don't understand."

"You can always make a background." He looked both sad and embarrassed. "In everybody's life there is, goodness knows, enough material."

Francesca, who had packed up her house and prepared to depart for her holiday in Brittany that she had taken every year (wars permitting) since 1936, could perhaps have supplied a background if they had asked her.

"Oh you amateur psychiatrists," cried Joanna. "You make me mad. You don't understand Ted."

She drummed on the table. As a doctor she felt the need to know accurately, to have the results of precise observation. But all the rules and training of her background rose up against it. You *don't*, not in Joanna's precise ordered society, go to a psychiatrist and say, "Is my young man a psychopath?"

You listened to your judgement, and your own judgement told you that Ted was a normal but talented young man.

Gene watched.

In the middle of the night Gene asked himself what it was he had done to Ted. Then he realised he didn't know what he had done to Ted. But it was what he must do. Sometimes events outran you. Sometimes you control them, sometimes they control you.

He turned over, curled up, and went to sleep.

Chapter 2

Enter Miss Mouse

A SMALL BROWN FIGURE scuttled down the narrow street leading to Ted's studio. She was a little quiet lady dressed in brown, like a little brown mouse. She carried a big bag slung over one shoulder from which she was handing out packets of a new detergent and then asking people to fill in a little questionnaire. Ted's studio was a poor choice to make. But you could bet it was a thing that had happened frequently to Little Brown Mouse. She was instinctively a bad chooser.

She looked around her. Certainly this was the place where she had seen *her*. She had looked in through the window and there, after ten years, she was.

Joanna let her in. For a second she and Joanna stared at each other. Each half-recognised the other. Joanna because she had, in fact, once seen the other woman before, but could not recall where and how. Little Brown Mouse because for a moment Joanna's

27

professional manner asserted itself She knew all about doctors.

She raised her eyes shyly as she came in. But underneath her shyness she was looking anxiously round the room. She wanted to say, "What have you done with my friend, you wicked girl? Where is she?" But she did not. She knew that way was danger: hands gently pressing you in one direction, voices saying quietly "*Now* Miss Brown, a prick and then sleep." So she bit back the words and instead gave a nervous sniff. She put down her bag.

"Oh I got one last week," said Ted cheerfully. "Found it on the doorstep. I don't rate another one. And what's more," he said even more cheerfully, "I've still got it." He dug under a heap of clothes and produced a battered but still unopened packet of 'Whito'.

Little Brown Mouse opened and shut her mouth in disappointment. Maybe it was disappointment.

"Oh I'll have another," said Ted, anxious not to disappoint.

Joanna was gentle with the little creature. She had recognised her now.

When Joanna had been a student this woman had come into a clinic where she was observing. It had been a psychiatric clinic. She vaguely remembered her symptoms and her name. Brown it was, or possibly Martin.

But that didn't mean the woman was mad. Far from it. In her way she had a sharp penetrating lucidity. You could see it on her face now.

"I'm enquiring for a friend," she said hesitantly. "I understand she's been here."

"Eh?" said Ted, blinking.

"You understand?" queried Joanna.

There was a pause.

"Well, I *saw* her," said Little Brown Mouse defensively.

Ted and Joanna met each other's eyes. "Be tactful," signalled Joanna silently. "What sort of a person is your friend?" she asked. Possibly it was Miss Osborne or Mrs. Barley from farther down the road.

"Have a cig?" said Ted.

She looked at it suspiciously then took one. "Well, I will. My favourite sort. I like the smell."

Over the smoke the Little Brown Mouse described her friend. A woman of her own age ('late forties', thought Joanna). Fair hair, spectacles, very well-dressed, worldly, clever. Little Brown Mouse seemed to have a tremendous admiration for her friend. She was vague about where they had actually known each other, although precise Joanna understood this vagueness and guessed it had been some mental clinic.

While the Little Brown Mouse talked Joanna summed her up. "I don't know what I ought to do," she worried. "It may be necessary to her find this woman. If she exists." "Leave it," said cold selfishness. "Have to," said reason. But life wasn't going to leave it. In a little while it was going to give the whole process a tweak.

29

"Which house did you actually see her in?" asked Ted.

There was a pause. "I saw her *here*," said Little Brown Mouse, mildly, firmly. "I saw her looking *out*."

They could not shake her. She argued but was obstinate.

"And I tell you what," she said over her shoulder, defiantly, as a parting shot, "I saw her. *And she saw me*."

Joanna sat drinking coffee in the Lyons in Cornmarket. It was not a fashionable place to drink. The *enfants dorés* of Oxford went across the road to the Roman splendours of the Espresso Bar, except for a group of choosey Etonians who felt lost and homeless and vaguely shocked to find there was *another* world outside Eton and other values besides m'tutor and m'dames and therefore clustered together; they took their breakfast here every morning.

Joanna drank her coffee and tightened her waistband. She had lost weight, and she knew it did not suit her. "Still, a waist is a waist," she consoled herself, as her mother had often pointed out to her. Her mother took the art of being beautiful very seriously indeed. As well she might, having built up a small fortune out of the London and New York Institute for Beauty Culture. She was almost, very nearly, an international name, and was responsible for various celebrated and even royal *maquillages*. You saw her faces, as it were (and they were the best faces), at royal weddings and coronations, and if there was a certain similarity, it was because Mrs. Duffy trusted her taste and not her clients' and didn't believe in letting them get out of hand. At least she let them vary it from year to year. There was always a new Duffy look. She brought out a new face once a year, timing it somewhere between the Dior and Balenciaga showings. Sometimes it was pretty much the old face, and sometimes it was so utterly different that the Duke of Wessex failed to recognise his own wife and invited her out to dinner on the strength of it, which was very embarrassing for both of them. At intervals she would get her hands on Joanna and then Joanna would go round for a few weeks wearing the New Duffy face and none of her friends would recognise her. But Joanna always lapsed back like a hedge that isn't trimmed often enough.

Joanna's mother didn't care for her daughter's chosen profession. "No chance of a girl being seen much in a mortuary, is there?"

"I suppose you think I ought to marry," said Joanna.

"Oh no, not necessarily," replied Mrs. Duffy seriously. "Marriage is sometimes quite disadvantageous to a woman's looks." She was thinking of several famous complexions she had repaired after the ravages of marriage and passion.

"A *quiet* life is best for a girl."

'Well, I get that,' thought Joanna.

Her father, who was a distinguished and indeed famous lawyer in London, equally disapproved of her activities as grubby and funereal, but he made no pretence of Beauty for Beauty's sake. "What you ought to do, my dear," he advised, "is to make a good marriage. Gives you status... Marriage," he observed oracularly, "gives you a position and prevents you keeping it up..." She knew he was a little soured about marriage owing to the frequent absences of his wife, whom he adored. As the years passed, she found that inspiration for her new faces made constant travel necessary. In the years after the war she had found a source in the Middle West of America. "But that fountain has run dry now," she complained and was driven south to Africa and north-east to the Himalayas. Questionable, really, if she wasn't remodelling the whole Indo-European countenance, and if she might not prove to be as influential in the long run as the invading Tartar, or the discoverer of America.

Joanna knew what her family meant. She could make a good marriage. She was not lovely enough, or worldly enough, or determined enough to make a brilliant match. The few remaining dukes were not for her, but she could marry into the group of families which served Queen and Country at home and abroad with distinction.

"But I want to do something useful," she cried.

"Oh yes," sighed her father. "Our family have

always had an irresistible urge to public service."

Joanna knew he was thinking of his brother, the diplomat. "You keep out of marrying into the Foreign Service, my girl" observed her old ex-Ambassador uncle, who lived in Oxford. "Does something rotten to a woman's character in the end. Nearly always end up writing a *book*." He was thinking, as they both knew, of his own newly published memoirs hanging fire while his wife's went into their 31st edition.

Ted, Joanna knew, was going to meet with no approval, from either side: he was neither an aid to beauty nor an establishment. At the moment he hardly looked like a husband.

As Joanna sat there mulling over these thoughts she became aware that someone was studying her. Across the room by the window and partly shielded by a sleepy Etonian eating a late breakfast, sat the Little Brown Mouse. She was staring hard at Joanna, willing her to look that way. For a moment Joanna pretended not to see. 'I know exactly what I'm going to do,' she thought miserably, 'in a little while I'm going over there and I'm going to let her talk to me.' She caught the woman's eyes and at once the anxious face was covered with a smile and she came over to Joanna.

"Hello," said Joanna. "Did you find your friend?" Brown Mouse had slipped a little since Joanna had seen her those few days ago. She was carrying her big bag but it was empty of packets and her hat was a little crooked. The hand that carried a cup of coffee was not quite clean.

"Not yet." She looked sad.

"We really didn't know who she was," said Joanna politely.

"No. You didn't perhaps, miss, said Little Brown Mouse politely. "Doctor, isn't it really? No, you didn't. But he did. He must have done. Why should he lie to me?"

Joanna stared at her. Miss Brown leaned forward.

"I saw her as clearly as I see you now, standing in the window, wearing a red and grey striped dress."

Joanna let herself into Francesca's great empty house, where she lived. It was very quiet with Francesca away for the summer. But this she welcomed, for she had much to think about. She sat down at her window. The house was a monument of Victorian Gothic with a touch of Venetian. She lived in one of twin towers, the right hand turret (the left had been pronounced dangerous), so that she felt like a bat, or a Charles Addams character. Far away in the basement Joanna could hear an angry cat voice. It was Mr. Kipps the cat. He was coming upstairs complaining. She went over to her door and called.

"Up here, Kipps old boy."

They kept each other company. Except for the cat Joanna was alone in the house.

She sat for a time again thinking. There was

something she ought to do but which she was frightened to do.

Through the window, pensively watching like the lady of Shallott, she could see in the ground floor kitchen of the house opposite her neighbour, Mr. Shardloes. He was one of her uncle's old friends, an old journalist. She knew and loved him. She also knew his puss Bonny who hated Mr. Kipps with the undying burning hate of one un-neutered tom for another.

His kitchen was being painted in pale blue and he was silhouetted against it. He was doing it himself and even from where she was sitting Joanna, who had excellent sight, could see he was doing it all wrong. "Mr. Shardloes, Mr. Shardloes," she wanted to shout, "start over by the window or you'll get stuck." But Mr. Shardloes was deaf and would never hear. Presently she saw Mr. Shardloes stand up and start to hop about as if he understood. Reassured by the normality of the sight, for everything Mr. Shardloes did had this quality of dottiness, and how he ever survived for thirty odd years as a special correspondent of *The Times* was a wonder, she got up and went over to her cupboard which was what she had wanted and feared to do.

She opened the door. It was full of clothes, a good many the present of her mother but a few Joanna's own choice. She reached her hand in and felt silk. Slowly she drew out a light-weight grey and red striped dress of which she and Ted were particularly fond.

She held it against her and looked in the mirror. "A grey and red striped dress," she heard the Little Brown Mouse mutter. 'Oh Ted, Ted,' she thought.

It was a beautiful and unusual dress. The silk was silver really and not grey, with a deep pink, had come from Paris and the workmanship was French, the label in the waistband had an address near the Place Vendôme. It had been the present of the year from Joanna's mother. It suited Joanna and brought out the colour in her pale dark skin.

It was a favourite dress with Ted and Gene. And it was, moreover a dress which had spent last week in Ted's studio. He had asked to borrow it, she had assumed, for a painting. "Lend it to me, Joanna, it stimulates me," he had said.

She rallied her reason and instructed herself it was because one only saw half the facts that there was this puzzle. If one knew more, understood better, there would be a rational, a substantial, real explanation of these mysteries. Uneasily it came to her that the reasonable explanation of the facts might also be an unpleasant one.

Resolutely Joanna turned back to her work. She was preoccupied with a type of virus disease affecting the new-born, and which in these tiny infants, inevitably resulted in death. It now seemed definitely established that it entered the system through the respiratory system, that it originated in a fleeting and unnoticed attack there which promptly migrated to the stomach. This being so it looked as though once it had been recognised in its earlier stages it should be easily dealt with. But Joanna had to admit that at the moment she had not the faintest idea how. As far as her own work was concerned she had done all that was demanded of her: she had traced the origin and behaviour of a group of virus diseases in relation to the newborn. This was her own private war.

Joanna, turning restlessly in her sleep that night, dreamt that she had solved the problem of her virus disease, then the solution—it had something to do with water—as is the way with dreams, slipped tantalisingly into limbo.

The very next day Ted appeared on her doorstep very early, before Mr. Kipps had come back from his early morning walk. He was carrying a knapsack and looked very clean and scrubbed. He gave her a warm kiss.

"I'll be better if I clear off for a few days," he said. "I need to be alone."

Joanna nodded. She didn't trust herself to say the right thing and she could see that he was emotionally wound up.

"Where are you going?" she said eventually.

"London. I'll write. Goodbye, Joanna."

She had one postcard from Ted, which came from London and said: "Work going well. News soon. And love."

So the hot summer days rolled by. A week passed, then nearly two. Oxford was empty of students, Francesca away, Gene off, the typing agency shut till September, Ted silent, in London. Little Brown Mouse disappeared too.

Joanna worked in her aseptic white world alone, speaking to her colleagues but hardly seeing them.

Then one day Joanna sitting over her breakfast read in her newspaper that a woman's body had been discovered in a trunk in a studio in St. Ebbe's Vale.

She read it without surprise, almost as if this was what she had been expecting.

Chapter 3

A Chinese Puzzle

IT WAS LIKE A CHINESE PUZZLE, in St.
Ebbe's was a flat, in the flat was a trunk, and in the
trunk was a body. The body of a woman.

The body had been discovered early in the
morning, or late the night before, depending how
you looked upon it, by the caretaker of the flats, of
which the studio, which she was paid to do once a
week only, was the last unconsidered bit. She had
gone in to clean. She had thought the room stuffy
and when an open window failed to clear it she
had investigated. Joanna remembered her well. She
was a decent woman.

The one thought she could not pass over, the
thought that would keep returning, was that Ted
had lived there with the body in the trunk.

The first thing was to get hold of Ted: he never
looked at a newspaper. It was so important to get
him here first. There was only one address to try in

London, he had terribly few friends there; but he had one, a man who taught at the Art School with him.

She telephoned. Only then with the bell ringing did she remember that the man rather disliked her.

A voice answered sleepily.

"Is Ted there?" asked Joanna bluntly, too anxious to go into circumstances.

There was a moment of silence, then, "No, should he be?"

The man sounded surprised.

"This is important, Alan, or I wouldn't ring now. Do you know where he is?"

Again a pause.

"Sorry. I'm not really awake. No, Ted isn't here, hasn't been here. And I don't know where he is."

Joanna put down the receiver.

And then because the living—or in her case the hope for the living—must come before the irrevocably dead, Joanna went to work at the hospital. She was trained by family tradition and education to a firm self-discipline, and to a code of values. She had concentrated on the work to be done. Joanna was anyway a person of great unselfishness and not inclined to concentrate on herself for long. She was not impulsive, but absorbed, serious, gentle. The familiar wave of smell greeted her, compounded of ether, disinfectant, health and sickness. She loved it. On the way to her laboratory far away from the medical and surgical blocks, she passed the long

40

corridor leading to the maternity and paediatrics block. Leonie Lamond was standing there.

"Hello," she said, holding herself well away. Joanna was constantly obsessed with the idea that she might somehow pass on a contact with the virus she worked with all the day and so she never went near a child or baby. In this case it seemed worth while keeping away from Leonie and Leonie's baby. So little, so fragile, so much loved.

"Another half-ounce," said Leonie, with her brown, radiant smile, "at this rate I'll have her home before the end of the month."

In the Path. Lab. Joanna quietly examined her post and made arrangements for her work to release her for a few hours. Her immediate boss, a woman much older than she, gave her a sharp look as she worked, but said nothing. She left the room and returned in a few minutes with a cup of coffee.

"Here, take this, it's terrible coffee but the idea is comforting. You can't expect a hospital canteen to be worldly enough to make good coffee, but what a contribution to the suffering of the world it would be if they could!" She returned to her work, deliberately not looking at Joanna. There was a deep friendship and trust between them.

"They make gorgeous tea, though," said Joanna weakly after a few minutes.

"You'd better get down to St. Ebbe's," said Alice, without looking up from her work. She, too, had read the newspapers.

St Ebbe's Vale was a terrace of sedate little Oxford houses, once entirely the province of college servants and still inhabited by a few although the dons were creeping in, as a bright turquoise or yellow door showed. Joanna knew that at the end of the road, next door to his father's butler, lived the eldest son of the Master of Mark's College and his charming Japanese wife, about whose marriage the whole of Oxford was agog. For the McNabs were all six feet tall and over, with bright red hair and irascible temperaments, and how would the Mendelian genes cope with that?

Ted's studio (so-called—it was one room with a skylight and a place for luggage) was right at the end abutting on a laundry. Ted didn't know it, but the girls in the laundry took an intense interest in him and admired him extremely, mostly on account of his lean and hungry look and knew more about his habits than Ted did himself. Ted couldn't have given you the name of his baker or his milkman but they could have told him. The police found this very useful later on when they were trying to build up a good picture of Ted.

A big black police car was standing at the end of the road parked up against the blank brick wall that hid the laundry. A uniformed constable stood discreetly by. Otherwise there was no sign of life. This didn't mean that St. Ebbe's Vale was uninterested, or uninstructed, Joanna knew better than that. But St. Ebbe's Vale was used to a backstairs, quiet, discreet way of showing its interest. When the President of St. Luke's fell in love for the first (and the last) time at the age of seventy, the kitchen and buttery staff and scouts (the old name for the college servants) knew all about it well before anyone else, and went on knowing all the details. But naturally they didn't say. It was the same now. St. Ebbe's Vale stood on Mark's College ground, the houses were all leased from it, it was an extension of the College, so, although full of an intense interest, no one was going to talk.

A tall thin-legged, red-haired figure left the house at the end of the road and disappeared round the corner without a backward glance at the police car. Even Joanna's gloom recognised it as a splendid figure. She saw the little black-haired figure of his wife at the window. Louise, all Oxford called her Louise, gave her something between a wave and a summons.

"Oh, do come in, Joanna," she said, "you must give me advice."

"I can't stop now," called Joanna, "back soon..."

"Oh, but it's the Ladies' Dinner," cried Louise, "shall I wear..."

Joanna waved and went on. Louise wouldn't take her advice anyway, let her sort the clothes out. She'd undoubtedly wipe the eye of all the Oxford matrons there anyway.

She tapped tentatively at the door of the house next door to Ted's studio. Number Ten. There was nothing smart and contemporary about Number Ten. It was good and solidly decorated with a big geranium in window and a mongrel black-and-white terrier sitting barking in the window. Cocky was an old friend, or enemy, of Joanna's and had once nipped her ankles walking down Cornmarket. "Just in fun," said Mrs. Brodie his mistress but Joanna didn't think it was in fun, she thought Cocky felt like it. Fortunately she had been wearing good, English-country lisle stockings and the injury had been more to her pride than anything else. They were not really dog lovers at Number Ten but Mrs. Brodie had inherited Cocky from a former employer, Miss Cartwright, second head of St. Ursula's College, who had died over ninety, near senile, but game and gay to the last, still fighting for women's suffrage absently forgetting that *that* battle was won and another started. "Miss Cartwright was a lady," was Mrs. Brodie's constant comment. A remark which, as it implied very few other people were, never failed to irritate Joanna. She knew *she* only won favour because her father was third cousin to an earl on the distaff side. Mrs Brodie had been cook at the establishment of learning where Joanna had taken her pre-medical studies. She was bedridden now and lived with her daughter and son-in-law, a gloomy man who worked in the Oxford Post Office. Between them they covered most of the news and intelligence of Oxford.

No one thought the daughter, Emily, had an easy life but it was agreed she had an interesting one with unrivalled opportunities for knowledge. Rumour had it that Emily was far from trodden-on and sought a wildly riotous life of pleasure at the local whist club.

Emily opened the door. Cocky emerged yapping. "Quiet, Cocky. Friends, boy, friends."

"So called," said Joanna, thinking of that ankle. She led the way into the neat little front parlour, everything shining and clean except where Cocky's privileged bottom had worn a dark patch on the window seat. Cocky jumped up there again, baring his teeth reminiscently at Joanna as he did so.

"Tell her to come up," shouted a stentorian voice from above. If Mrs. Brodie had weakened it had not been in the lungs.

"Mother wants you," whispered Emily; she always whispered about Mother although the noise Mother made was frequently deafening and a psychologist would have said that this was perfectly straightforward defence mechanism: that Mrs. Brodie was a little deaf and that consciously or unconsciously Emily was getting her revenge.

Upstairs the old lady, with her Mrs. Beaton by her side and Mrs. Fanny Mason's cookbook on her lap (for she still kept up her interests) turned a sharp eye on Joanna.

"Of course I know why you've come."

45

"We had Mrs. Lace in here," said Emily with mild
pride. "Terrible upset she was. Wanted to telephone.
But of course we haven't got a telephone here. 'I
believe there's a body in that trunk,' she said. 'I
think you must be mistaken, dear,' I said to her.
However it turned out she wasn't."

The biggest lump of news in St. Ebbe's Vale for
years, bigger by far than when the Rector of St.
Jerome's had eloped with his typist, had fallen into
their laps, and they were in a state of suppressed
excitement.

"What do you know about it, Mrs. Brodie?"
asked Joanna, confident of a plain statement of the
facts.

The body had been discovered in the trunk early
in the morning by the police constable eventually
fetched by the cleaner. No one but the constable
had seen anything then, because he immediately
locked the door and fetched assistance. No one in
St. Ebbe's Vale saw anything later, because the trunk
and its contents were afterwards removed by
special van. The cleaner had, however, supplied the
news that it was a big brown trunk and had been
partly covered by an old travelling rug belonging
to Mr. Ted Roman, which looked as though it had
slipped off.

Very soon however the news had spread through
the constable's wife, through the constable's wife's
sister, through the constable's wife's sister's brother,
who worked in the Post Office side by side with

Mrs. Brodie's son-in-law, that the body was that of a woman, as far as they could tell, that it was curled up inside the trunk, and had been strangled with a ligature.

"A tie, we've heard."

In everything the body precisely paralleled the curious accidents that had already happened to Ted. The body was bound, it was crammed into a small space, it had been strangled. Only, unlike Ted, the job had come to a successful conclusion and she was dead.

"The Doctor's working on it now," said Mrs. Brodie.

"Yes," said Joanna. Well, she knew all about *that*. She knew the set routine, the order of procedure, just what they would do to the body. She probably even knew the doctor. She just didn't know the body, she hoped.

"I'm afraid it looks bad for Mr. Ted," said Mrs. Brodie. "He should never have gone away and left her, should he?" Mrs. Brodie spoke seriously and solemnly. Ted was already tried and found guilty.

"She can't have been a very nice woman," said Mrs. Brodie, "to have got herself into such a place."

"Oh, Mrs. Brodie…"

"But he didn't ought to have left her. Besides, it'll go against him, won't it? Can't say it was an accident or anything like that."

"He's been away," protested Joanna, "and the body was found early this morning."

47

"Oh no," Mrs Brodie spoke briskly. "Not today. Day before. Police said to keep quiet until they said."

The police had kept the murder quiet for nearly thirty-six hours.

"I wonder why?" said Joanna.

"Trying to lay their hands on someone," speculated Mrs. Brodie. "In any case, there's something funny about this murder. I'm telling you straight."

The interview was over. Mrs. Brodie turned back to her books. Joanna suspected she was partly identifying herself with her late boss Miss Cartwright, because her attitude to cooking was becoming more and more scholarly, she was always collating recipes and discussing the origin of pasta. The joke was that she had never been a very good cook, all her food being pleasant to look at but tasting much the same, and rather chilly and tepid.

Emily had something to say.

"You know Mother doesn't sleep much these days. Watches out of the window a good deal." This was an understatement. Mrs. Brodie watched all the time and even had a mirror fixed up at a special angle, a kind of periscope.

Joanna nodded.

"Mother never saw that woman, never saw any woman come there at all," whispered Emily.

"She could have missed her."

"I know. Even Mother drops off sometimes. But not during the day. And the last few weeks she has only slept in the small hours. Mother says she never saw a woman go down past us."

Joanna shrugged.

But Emily stuck to her point. "I just don't see how she got here, that's all," she said obstinately.

Then she dropped her voice. "You don't think he *brought* her there in the trunk already?" she said.

But Joanna knew that one person claimed to have seen the woman in the studio and she wondered what Little Brown Mouse was making of the news. If she even knew of it.

It would be possible perhaps to track down Miss Brown if she really tried. It would mean going back in her memory and recalling definitely the time and date (and that took you back about four years now) when Miss Brown's case had been studied at the clinic where she was a student. She would then have to get permission to study the records for the patient's name and address.

An hour and a half later Joanna was almost willing to give up.

Name
Age
Address
Case History
Prognosis

She thumbed through the pages. There seemed

nothing there. And then suddenly Joanna remembered it all vividly. She had sat in on this clinic and taken detailed notes for the benefit of her then boyfriend, a rugger Blue from Corpus who had since turned miraculously into an ear nose and throat surgeon and whom Joanna still saw occasionally. Now she knew what to look for, and found it quickly.

Prognosis: Fair. She frowned. She knew what *that* meant. The chances were better than average that Miss Brown would be back in the clinic's hands again and again and again.

It also meant that one had to ask oneself: How reliable was Miss Brown as a witness? She might on some points be an accurate reporter and observer; on others, not to be trusted. What had she really seen?

The house where Miss Brown lodged was not typical of Oxford or not at least what the stranger thinks typical of Oxford, it was a small red brick house in a side street of Cowley. It might have been a house in any industrial city and reminds you that Oxford is in fact in the Midlands of England and has a population of thousands of workers. Joanna was glad, really, to find Miss Brown so comfortably housed because there had been about her the indefinable look of someone who gets the worst of conditions everywhere. In this she was not entirely wrong as she discovered once inside the house, which had a desolate grubby look of near-poverty. It looked nicer outside than it did in. Miss Brown had a room on the top floor. On the door was a small card: Miss Martin Brown.

It was still early and she had every hope of finding her quarry at home. She knocked at the door. There was no answer. Indeed the whole house seemed empty and still. But there was a savoury smell of cooking coming from beyond the door and that encouraged her. She knocked again, and this time a voice called out.

"Come in, you are early. I heard the first time, but I was dishing up and I thought you would just walk in."

There was a happy confident note of welcome in Miss Brown's voice that Joanna knew she was going to dissipate and she hated herself for doing. She went in slowly. Miss Brown was standing by a gas stove in the far corner of the room stirring a saucepan. She looked up with a smile that faded. Carefully she laid down the spoon and took the pan from the flame.

"You didn't expect me," said Joanna. It was not a question.

"Come in," said Miss Brown blankly. "Ask what you want and go quick. You are from the factory, I suppose?"

'She doesn't recognise me', Joanna thought. 'She doesn't recognise me…'

"Tell them, no. I do not work for them any more. I have another job, a better one, and if they want their packets of tiresome soap powder, tell them they can have them. I don't use it."

"I've not come about the soap powder."

51

"The man with the motor-car then? It was an accident. I did not mean to kick him."

Joanna shook her head. "Not even that..." But her heart was sinking. How could she trust whatever answer she got here? For Betty Martin-Brown was in for one of her spells "I came to ask you about the woman—your friend—that you asked me about before. You remember in St. Ebbe's?"

"Oh. Well, you look different" said Miss Brown. "You shouldn't wear a hat. It doesn't suit you. People with round faces should never wear hats." This recommendation, an exact reproduction of advice often given by Joanna's mother, was a reminder that Miss Brown could be sharp enough when she pleased.

"About the woman, your friend," began Joanna. Sanity, lucid and possessed, flooded into Miss Brown's eyes. It carried conviction She shook her head. "No,' she said. "I made a mistake. I didn't see her. She has been dead for over ten years."

"Wait. Think a minute. You seemed so sure before."

"No," she said almost viciously.

Joanna accepted her defeat gamely.

"Here is my address if you ever want me." She gave Miss Brown her card. The card which she had had made in a flash of *hubris* when she first qualified. "Joanna Duffy, B.A., M.B., Ch.B."

Miss Brown took it and twisted it in her hands as if she might tear it up. But she did not. Instead she

52

popped it on the shelf, next to a china dog, and the packet of cigarettes Ted had given her. It was the same packet because of the way Ted always wrenched the top off. Miss Mouse had smoked a few but not many.

On the staircase Joanna met the landlady. "I was calling on Miss Brown," she said. "I don't think she's too well."

The woman nodded. She seemed to understand, although not to show passionate interest. "I'll pop in."

"Who was she expecting?"

"I don't think she was expecting anyone," said the woman awkwardly. "She does that all the time." She looked slightly irritable. "It's awkward, you know. Sometimes she's cooking cabbage at twelve o'clock at night."

Cooking cabbage for someone who never came. What a sad hell. It seemed a shame Miss Brown couldn't have been granted a happier madness. But there it was again—she really was a woman who got the worst of everything. Joanna knew a woman whose delusions took the form of believing herself Marilyn Monroe. She was wildly, deliriously happy, her state of euphoria complete.

Before she got home Joanna telephoned the woman who had charge of the out-care mental patients. "Oh yes, I know about Miss Brown," she said with a sigh. "I'll go round. Nice of you to telephone. I don't know what started this last thing off. She was going along nicely."

'It might have been a dead woman,' thought Joanna macabrely as she rang off. A woman who had been dead for ten years.

'Did she go in the trunk,' another voice had asked, 'that poor dead woman?'

But she had walked there, in fact, the woman Joanna and Mrs. Brodie were talking of, had walked there on her own two feet as she usually did. She had even seen Mrs. Brodie, but it had meant of course, nothing. It was supremely natural she should walk down St. Ebbe's Vale and as a matter of course she often did it. Yes, and Mrs. Brodie saw her. On this occasion she had walked there in a state of excitement which she did not often get into these days. She feared it must show through. And it was all due to Joanna and a red dress. The dress reminded her of a dress she had once known and loved. Not on herself but on another. Red had never suited her sturdy shape and odd dark skin. But you do sometimes covet precisely what is not for you, and she knew that she wanted to wear the red and grey dress. Which was the biggest surprise of all.

She was drawn to the studio by an itch to paint, a legitimate impulse, no need to hide it, but with it went impulses less easy to control and, she knew, dangerous. It was funny after years and years of doing what seemed the right thing for her to be back in a muddle again. Painting was perhaps a form of exhibitionism and she knew or judged herself to be an exhibitionist. She knew the patter of psychology. Who better?

On the way there, a little crisis occurred of the kind she met often. St. Ebbe's Vale was not a street she cared for. A long struggle to support herself to be the breadwinner to be the man of the family (*and* the woman too) had produced a strong desire for luxury, ease, lavishness, and the quiet respectability of St. Ebbe's Vale made no appeal. If you're obliged to be the man of the family you suddenly get absolutely fed up with it and want to be indulged. (There was however small chance of anyone doing any indulging.) And this want came out in funny, funny ways.

She saw a child dancing. Being a South Oxford child she was dancing clumsily and heavily, but it was a genuine moment of gaiety.

Restrain the gesture, restrain the gesture—you should always avoid the spectacular she told herself regretfully. Magnificence rarely pays. She threw the child a penny. The child turned, open-mouthed, unaware that it was really a shower of roses you were throwing, or a silver penny in a Roman fountain. The mother rushed forward, muttered, and led the child away.

But it was one more step down into depression. A feeling that somewhere back a wrong choice had been made. Loving is not always synonymous with living nor is love always stronger than fear.

It was just about then that the point of her dream

flashed back into Joanna's mind. For a moment she anxiously wondered whether there could be any validity in it. Then she turned her feet back to her work bench. As she crossed the entrance of the hospital she saw in the distance the tall thin figure of Father Mahoney, the priest from St Ebbe's known to all his parishioners as Father Maarney. Vaguely she wondered why he was here.

"You here?" said Alice

"Come back to work," said Joanna slipping into her white coat.

"Good. Phoebe cut her hand so she's had to go off."

"Oh, dangerous?" said Joanna. But all cuts were dangerous in their work.

"A scratch," Alice sounded preoccupied. "Police rang up asking for you."

"Oh, what did you say?"

"That you were out."

Alice straightened up. "But they'll telephone again I'm afraid."

"It's Ted they're after" said Joanna in a stony voice. Alice hesitated, then she said "I may be wrong, but I sort of got the idea that they thought *you* might know the dead woman.

Joanna dropped in at the Medical School Library and turned into the wing dealing with psychiatry.

If she was to help Ted she must know.

Her father had once said to her "You may not have a better case than your opponent, you may

56

not be a mind-reader able to know beforehand how they will attack your case, but you must always know more than they do: more law, more background, more information about the characters."

She must know more now.

It was not a section Joanna had troubled about much as a student, because you can't after all, cover everything, and even then she had been fascinated by the complexity of viruses, and a little cautious and sceptical before a discipline which seemed to her more of an art than a science. "How could you," she asked, "claim to know so much about the human mind when your own mind is itself the perceiving instrument."

But now the section seemed to welcome her. One or two people were working there but they took no notice of her. Jung, Adler, Freud. She ran her hand along the shelves seeking for the definitive work. She soon found one, Miller and Geddes (Oxford, 1948), *Psychology and Mental Health.*

She sat down and bent over it, turning straightway to the chapters on Obsessions and Compulsions: their origins and nature. "Another large group of functional disturbances, hysterical in their nature, obsessional and compulsive, are linked together under the phrase 'psychopathic personality,'" she read. "These illnesses are ones in which the patient develops impulses to behave in certain ways which he cannot ignore and to which he must yield, although he recognises them to be both abnormal and really to be resisted. Dr. Johnson found himself obliged to touch every lamp post he passed (not such a job in eighteenth-century London, one supposes, as it would be now) There is the little boy who *has* to say a prayer every morning before school. And there is the nurse who feels she must strike the patient she is tending. A true obsessional patient will always be able to control this impulse. The schizophrenic is all too likely to obey."

"How do you know the difference?" wondered Joanna, scribbling notes on a paper. Obsessional patients tend to get depressed, and suicidal. This query was strengthened in her by the information she read later that obsessional symptoms are not uncommonly the means by which other more serious mental illnesses such as schizophrenia manifest themselves.

She considered her notes thoughtfully.

Danger, danger, danger, rang the little warning bell in her brain.

Finally she read: "Agoraphobia. The need to be in a tight dark place. Back to the womb, e.g. often associated with tying up with strings and braces, cf. to umbilical cord. Probably sexual in origin but often to be associated with a profound mental shock in childhood."

She gathered her notes together and stood up. The librarian watched her go out.

She weighed all this up against what she knew

of Ted and still she could not make the two sides
match.

Chapter 4

Miss Rosa Mantle

FOR A TIME THE DEAD WOMAN had masqueraded, through no fault of her own, under the name of Rosa Mantle. As Rosa Mantle she was sought by the police in the Borough, South-East London. They had traces of her as living in Czar Passage, in Little Poland Street, off Tower Bridge Road.

This at once brought her within the orbit of John Coffin, Londoner, Detective Inspector and man of steel, with all the malleability, high friction content and obduracy of high quality steel. He was also a man with a conscience, and his conscience was troubled now. He knew as well as he knew anything that something was now going on in his manor, that it had to do with fiddling the wine coming through the docks and that profit was not the main motive but the big Smith-Cordory wedding that was coming off soon. He considered the personalities involved. Big John Smith, Old Man

Cordory. Then he made up his mind. He would attend the wedding.

It wasn't perhaps a good thing to do, but it was the best thing he could think of in the circumstances. Anyway, they would know he knew.

He sat and thought for a while about other circumstances. It was funny. You went to school, you stayed at school (L.C.C. Boys School), on and off anyway. You left school, Mum was not pleased. You went to night school, Mum was pleased. You joined the Force, Mum was not pleased again. You walked the beat well, got promotion, Mum was pleased. You joined the detective branch and Mum was not pleased and talked about ratting. Mum's ancestry and her sympathies were dubious.

It would be wrong to say that Mum had criminal tendencies, but she was certainly against the Law. At the same time she was a proud mother and wanted you to shine at being DDI. She was pleased to be the mother of the youngest DDI in London, but she said it *marked* her among her friends. "They don't trust me," she said. And when you said choose different friends then the roof fell in.

It had fallen in last night. But mind you it had been sagging for some time anyway. There was Patsy. Cleopatra Mary Partridge, aged thirty-four, an actress, pretty and determined. Mother and Patsy were birds of a feather, really, and to be the son of one and to fall in love with the other was, while psychologically inevitable no doubt, bad luck.

It was a year now since Patsy, Cleopatra and Coffin had met and eleven months since Coffin had been engaged. Patsy, on the other hand, seemed still to be disengaged.

The tension had started as soon as they met, over a year ago now, in a murder case in Birmingham, where Coffin's first choice job had been to amass evidence which seemed to point strongly in favour of his love being a murderess. They had got on a see-saw then, both of them, and so far showed no sign of ever getting off.

Part of the trouble was that Patsy was a successful actress. If she had been a failed actress Coffin could have laid firm hands on her and brought her home to look after him, but you can't do this with a woman who is earning more than you are in a high-powered comedy with Venetia Stuart. They had started with *Wait for the Bride*, made a film called *Get that Bride*, and had now moved with *The Bride comes Home* to Oxford for the pre-London run. It looked like being the usual success. It could go on forever.

None of this would have mattered, as even successful actresses have the usual urges, but Patsy was not normal. "I'm gun shy," she said somewhat sourly (one of Patsy's vices was a streak of cynicism). "Look what's happened to me in the last few years. Fall in love with a man and it turns out he's an overgrown delinquent." She seemed nervous about the effect love might have on Coffin. So the affair was off, on, and off again. It was in a yellow light period at the moment with both parties taking time off. Mrs. Coffin, unpredictable and feminist as ever, took Patsy's side; and Coffin, although well fed, well housed and ministered-to, had been made to feel deprived of feminine support and cheer.

Then he sighed, rang his bell for the next job, and the problem of the identity of Rosa Mantle came in.

The Oxford Police, in the person of Inspector Peter Pinching, had sent the dead woman's fingerprints to the Central Bureau Scotland Yard; they, after some quick work, had produced the name of Rosa Mantle and suggested a contact with Coffin's Division, which had been her last known address. All this had happened speedily and Coffin had received the request for help many hours before Joanna opened her newspaper and read about the discovery of the body in St. Ebbe's. In fact by that time Coffin had already come up with a few answers.

He chewed it over silently to himself for a while. They had taken the fingerprints of the woman in the Oxford trunk; surprisingly, Scotland Yard had one record: petty shop lifting, 1950, address: Little Poland Street. Contacts and history please? "Yes," said Coffin to himself, "contacts and history ten years ago." He knew his Little Poland Street: a solid community of mind-your-own-businessmen with a floating population whose business was intimately connected, usually illegally, with other people's. The wide boys. If Poland Street remembered anything about Rosa Mantle and her friends they were not likely to say. He might send Mother down but he doubted if even she cut any ice in Little Poland Street.

Rosa Mantle's offence was petty, not a bad case, it was even an understandable one. Rosa Mantle had stolen books—English, French and German novels and biographies which she had no money to buy. It was true also that she did not always keep the books; those which on reading she thought poorly of were returned. Even the magistrate had admitted that she had chosen excellently. In fact it would certainly have counted strongly in her favour had not the irate bookseller pointed out that such returned books were invariably defaced with exclamation marks, rude comments, and torn-out pages.

It was a very ordinary sort of case, duplicated a thousand times over, probably, in all big cities and university towns. This had taken place in a big store in Oxford Street but even here it had not been remarkable; the manager admitted they had had many such over the years. Rosa Mantle had got off with a caution and a fine. The magistrate had added the suggestion that as she seemed to be in a very strung-up state she should see a doctor.

"Haven't they got anything newer on her?" he asked aloud. "And if not why not?" But there was nothing new in the records about Rosa, she had dropped out of sight. There was a point there, but it was not his point and he left it. He put on his hat and hurried round to Little Poland Street. There were one or two small matters he wanted to ask Little Poland Street on his own account anyway.

Little Poland Street saw him coming. While never actually seeming to be on the look-out for anything it rarely missed much. Czar Passage was at the end of Little Poland Street. It was a street of grey-brick little houses with flat faces and small windows, but out of these little windows plenty of eyes were always watching. It was difficult to believe that the Czar it commemorated was Peter the Great of Russia and that the forerunners of these dingy houses had been warehouses and homes of prosperous merchants of Caroline London. Little Poland Street did not remember its history—as indeed why should it?

He stopped outside No.3, the reputed address of Rosa Mantle, and gave a low whistle. He knew the occupants. It was one of the most irritating, for that matter the *most* irritating family, in Czar Passage. There were only four houses in Czar Passage, so the competition wasn't high but the Dove family would have won this title anywhere any time.

He rang the bell and rang it again. Eventually a tall thin man appeared.

"Why don't you keep your place cleaner, Dove?" said Coffin, giving the doorstep an irritable kick. Czar Passage, although not prepossessing, was clean enough; but No.3 was covered with greasy dirt and the remains of someone's fried fish supper. "Pooh, the smell."

"It's the smell of poverty, Inspector, the smell of poverty," said Mr. Dove, "the dirt's the result of my poverty. It is indeed."

Long ago Mr. Dove's grandparents had come from Wales and, although Mr. Dove himself had been born round the corner from Czar Passage in Lombardy Grove, he still retained a memory of his ancestors' home in his voice. A dim memory, well overlaid with cockney and a whine that was purely Dove, but the Welsh was there.

"See you've got a television set," said Coffin sourly, looking at the aerial and was then immediately ashamed of himself for saying it: the Doves were genuinely poor but why shouldn't they have a television set? But that was the thing about the Doves, they brought the worst out in you.

And even if it wasn't the smell of poverty, it was the smell of sickness. There was always someone sick in that house.

"Can I come in?" He gathered himself together to face the onslaught of the house on him; Coffin had a sensitive nose.

"We try to make everyone welcome," said Mr. Dove almost giving a bow, and at the same time booting out of the way a lean grey cat that was trying to get in and undoubtedly lived there. It had a Dove look. "Although mother's very bad."

"Oh, it's mother today, is it?" Coffin looked round

for somewhere to stand, he did not aspire or wish to sit, but even standing was difficult in that crowded room. Someone had upset a pail of dirty water, or perhaps it had been beer, and it still hung around in little puddles.

There was a low hooting noise in the background.

"Ah, she's heard you," said Mr. Dove listening. "She wants you to step up… That's not like Mother, she usually can't abide any face but mine when she's poorly, let alone a copper." He listened. "Ah, I'm wrong, she's asking you to get out…" He sounded relieved. "That's more like Mother."

Coffin shifted his feet uneasily. "How long have you been living here, Dove?"

"In this house Inspector? Since 1951. But it was in the possession before that of my dear Aunty and I was always in and out."

"Yes," said Coffin.

He remembered Aunty, although it was early days in the Division. Aunty was not a Dove but a Parrott and had been the late Mrs. Dove's elder sister. A charming Poll Parrott too, by all accounts, in her youth but a rough, tough old lady, with the habit of running up and down stairs shouting when she was angry, when Coffin got to know her. It was true, though, that she had kept lodgers.

"Did she ever have anyone here about that time, just before she died, called Rosa Mantle? Do you remember? You'd know, wouldn't you?"

There was no need to have pretences, to beat about the bush with the Doves, in their curious sort of way they were honest.

"Yes, I'd remember," said Dove, screwing up his eyes and putting on another pair of spectacles. Since the advent of the National Health Service both the Doves had had two or three pairs of spectacles. It was indeed their constant bad health that kept them going financially. It didn't make them rich but it saved them from starving.

"Aunty had rather a lot round then, they kept coming and going." He scratched his head. "She struck rather a rich seam by then. She put an advertisement in the *New Statesman* saying 'ten minutes from the City, thirty bob a week, only ladies of culture considered'. She got quite a few ladies. But of course they mostly didn't stay long."

"I can see that."

"Your Miss Mantle may have been one of them. We had a few that weren't ladies, too, I can tell you. But Aunty wouldn't stand for that. Was she respectable, your Miss Mantle?"

Coffin shrugged.

"Can't be, can she though?" continued Dove, thinking aloud, "if *you're* looking for her."

"She's dead," said Coffin shortly.

"Oh, I see."

Dove looked puzzled but helpful. "Got a bit more to go on?"

"We got her fingerprints sometime in April, 1950," said Coffin. "We picked her up for a petty offence. Address given as here."

The hooting upstairs had stopped and a steady

banging on the floor had taken its place.

"I'll just step up and put it to Mother," said Mr. Dove, "unless you care to come up yourself? She's pretty steady at the moment."

"No thank you," said Coffin, remarking that there was no lack of power behind the bangs.

He sat himself down and waited for a few minutes. Dove soon came down carrying a hot water bottle and a teapot.

"Mother says she doesn't know anything about the petty offence and the police, but Aunty had two ladies here together and one was called Rosa Mantle and the other Jeanie Low. But Mother says you're not to think from that that she was Scotch because she wasn't."

"And you can't remember anything else?"

"It was just before Aunty died, what she may have known we can't say, but she took it with her."

"Well, thanks. It doesn't look as though it'll do much good but I'll pass it on."

There was a shriek from upstairs and Mr. Dove rushed to the door. "What's that, Mother? Your hat? Oh no, Mother, you don't need your hat. Oh, wait a minute, Mother, I'll come up. What? Oh yes, Mother, I've got it now."

He darted from the room and returned in triumph a few minutes later with a round straw hat.

"Here, Mother says she had this hat from Miss Mantle. Miss Mantle left it behind. It's a good hat," he added with satisfaction.

Coffin looked at it. The years of Mrs. Dove had reduced the hat to a battered grey mass.

Then a thought struck him. "How big is your wife?" He asked knowing the answer.

"Five feet just," said Mr. Dove proudly. "Fairy, I used to call her. Tiny was her name in the family. Accounts for her being so delicate, she's too small."

"The hat a good fit?"

Mr. Dove went up to ask. "Splendid," he said. "Mother liked it. You can see she did."

"So I can," said Coffin. "Mind if I take it with me?" He watched it being wrapped up in an ancient newspaper. Mr. Dove sold newspapers on the corner of Little Poland Street and the Tower Bridge Road when he was strong enough.

He slid a note into Mr. Dove's hand as he departed. It was foolish maybe to do it but they certainly were poor and the hat, whatever it looked like, was a genuine link with Miss Rosa Mantle.

"Oh, thank you, Inspector," said Mr. Dove. "Your little contribution will be warmly welcomed by Mother." He gave the grey cat another kick as it made another attempt to get in. It was impossible to love the Doves.

So Coffin went back home to his office and consulted the information that had been sent him. He then collated this with what he had learnt from Mrs. Dove and the mute testimony of the hat.

Then he sent off a wire. "Probably not Mantle. May be Low. Look for Low."

So the dead woman was allowed to emerge from behind the mask she had assumed in a panic and because she feared the police, and was allowed to take up, for a moment, another name. She was now Miss Jeanie Low, who was *not* a Scot.

Chapter 5

Miss Jeanie Low

AS MISS JEANIE LOW, the dead woman had been pursued by Inspector John Coffin. With surprising results. Acting fast on information received from Mr. Dove, "that they were always in attendance at the hospital," he had covered, or caused to be covered, the big hospitals easily reached from Southwark. Most hospitals were, but he took a chance, followed the feeling in his bones and concentrated on one: The South London Hospital for Nervous Diseases.

Miss Low and Miss Mantle were traced there.

Now the dead woman came out a little from her hiding. They knew who she wasn't. She was not Miss Rosa Mantle, and they were that much nearer who she really was.

"It's enough," said Coffin, "she isn't Mantle, but she knew her. Was probably in fairly close contact.

72

Find Mantle and she'll identify the body. Probably as Jeanie Low. Both the names are false, of course."

Coffin, combining business with pleasure, had taken his information down to Oxford himself.

"I've got a direct lead on to her as it happens."

"You mean you know all there is to know already?" commented his Oxford colleague somewhat sourly. He already had a fairly good idea of Coffin's working methods. Still, it did some of his work for him.

"That's it," agreed Coffin radiantly. He had had a good day. "Nothing can go wrong for you, boy, today," he was saying inside. He had had a highly exhilarating, racy interview with Patsy, with no holds barred on either side, and although some people might have called it a flaming quarrel, he knew better, knew he had scored a point and felt a new man.

"I went down to the hospital and they came across with the info." He smiled widely.

"They had the couple of them there all right. Statistically matching, everything cosy, been in-patients and then outpatients, but they weren't called Mantle and Low. That pair of names they adopted for some rum reasons of their own, wanted to feel different; no, in hospital they went under their real names of Brown and Loeb.

"Miss Brown is said now to be in the Oxford area, and this is her address." He flipped over a piece of paper. It was the address of the Little Brown Mouse.

The Oxford Police Inspector gazed at the piece of paper.

"Well, thanks. Brown's a contact all right. Must be Low we've got in the trunk." Very rightly, he looked puzzled. He had a deep suspicion that in spite of Coffin's assurance, nothing was as simple as it seemed. He moved his hand to the telephone. "We'd better get on to Brown."

"I bet she's come your way before."

"She may have," said the local man thoughtfully.

Coffin leaned forward and tapped on the paper—a faint breath of Patsy's scent drifted across. "You study the facts I've got for you here. And then work out what you think some of the medical details mean." He leaned back, still confident.

"I'm glad you're here," said the Inspector, doubtfully, gloomily.

There was another fine-spun chain leading to John Coffin as Investigator. For some time past he had been, gradually, almost against his will, becoming a specialist in a certain kind of death. Deaths that were not quite what they seemed.

There was the young woman who had locked herself in a room and then drawn the curtains and drunk poison out of her own tooth glass, but who had in fact been murdered. The two women, one old, one young, who had wrapped themselves in rugs and sat in a car where they quietly asphyxiated from carbon monoxide, but who had, all the same, been murdered. The boy who had a broken neck but had in fact died by murder. The girl who had died from strangulation, and who yet had died peacefully by her own hand, a suicide and not murdered, with her eyes weighted down. The married couple who had driven themselves willingly, knowingly, over a dockside into the dirty Thames in a car, but who had not been suicides at all but had been murdered.

He was the specialist in the offbeat deaths. This position was becoming recognised outside London and he was often quietly called in to give advice. The pathologists and the technicians contributed the factual background of what could have happened but Coffin made the final assessment, weighing up what they said was possible with what he knew to be probable. He had started to say wryly that he could do with a good old-fashioned straightforward murder. He had read the reports of the Oxford murder and had rubbed his chin thoughtfully.

He was not surprised therefore when in response to his message about Rosa Mantle he had a telephone call suggesting he come down to see the body with the comment that this was 'just up his street'.

"Must think I live on Queer Street," he commented to himself. But it was true. In a sense he did. And it was one of the things Patsy had against him.

His Oxford colleagues had their comment too. "Probably prove to us she isn't dead at all," they joked. But nevertheless they showed him all the evidence they had and took the subsequent discussion seriously.

Coffin spent a long time studying the official photographs. He concentrated on the photograph of the body in the trunk. The body was curled up in the position in which it had died; a ligature was tied round the throat, a scarf cutting into the throat; a small handkerchief had been thrust into the mouth and tightly packed against the throat. The lid had been drawn down.

"Asphyxiated as much as strangled," said the Oxford Inspector shortly.

"Body's not in a bad state," commented Coffin.

"Not as much decomposition as you might expect," agreed Inspector Pinching. "Considering we estimate it's been there about two weeks. More mummified than anything."

Coffin studied the scarf from the dead woman's neck, which had been cut off with the knot intact, and the handkerchief, which had been thrust into the throat. The knot was a slipknot; the handkerchief had belonged to a man.

"I'd like to see the flat," he asked.

So Coffin was taken to St. Ebbe's. He inspected the room and the trunk.

He drew aside the curtain, which protected the alcove where clothes hung. There was very little there. Ted had taken most with him, leaving just a suit and a jacket. But hanging in the corner was a woman's dress.

Coffin raised his eyebrows expressively.

"Yes. I bet you've got it all sewn up here, boy."

His companion muttered something about the pathologist's report.

The room was dusty and cheerless, in the hot summer evening. It had the feel of a room in which something very terrible had happened. Whatever happened, no one would ever paint in this room again.

The police had gone over everything, yet had hardly disturbed anything. All the same the room was as finally and irretrievably altered as the earth is when it is dug: the ground may be planted over, crops may grow, generations and centuries come and go, but the character of the earth is changed forever. You can never quite put back what you have moved. So it was with Ted's room, it had always been untidy, it was disordered, always dirty, now it was sordid.

Coffin inspected the door, which showed no signs of having been broken in and which indeed could not be locked, although it had been wedged and the small piece of wood used to do this was still to be seen.

"Wouldn't hold against much," said Coffin.

"Wasn't needed to," said his colleague briefly. "Time wasn't a problem."

Coffin studied the trunk which had been replaced *in situ* for his benefit, although emptied of its contents. It was a big trunk, large and heavy. He raised and dropped the lid several times. It fell with a great weight like the guillotine.

He examined again Ted's clothes hanging up behind the dusty curtain. A tweed jacket and his one suit of town dark blue which looked as if it had first been made for Ted when he was sixteen and hardly been worn since. It was more of a symbol than a suit to Ted. It represented the outside conventional world into which he so rarely went but for which he had the right clothes if they were needed.

"We'd better get down to see Miss Brown, sometime Mantle. She is called Rosa, I suppose? No, I know," said Coffin. "Rose, that'll be it. Rose."

But Rose, by any other name, inscrutable, withdrawn Rose, was withheld from them.

"No, you cannot interview Miss Brown," said the Mental Health visitor. "You cannot speak to Miss Brown, you cannot even *see* Miss Brown. She is incommunicado, undergoing treatment," she explained briefly.

"But I will let you do something else. I will let you have the transcript of her story about her last interview with the dead woman."

Coffin looked interested.

"I think it will help you a good deal."

Chapter 6

Sybil's Contribution

IT WAS NOT THE POLICE who were waiting for Joanna in her turret room when she returned for a light and unwanted lunch. She let herself into the dark quiet hall with its smell of damp and green plants, noticing as she did so that the door was not locked and that there was a note from the woman who came in and cleaned for her and Francesca and had cleaned for Ted in the days when Ted lived there. She picked it up.

"Milk in fridge, cat food hidden in back kitchen in the game larder. The laundry didn't come and I believe they've lost yours, my dear Miss Duffy."

Mr. Kipps wound himself round Joanna's ankles, murmuring in a throaty voice something about the desirability of lunch. She picked him up and stroked him. "All right, food for you, old boy. Are you allowed out?" She looked out of the window.

A red flag was flying on the house across the way where Mr. Shardloes, the retired *Times* correspondent and his cat Bonny lived. She sighed. "No, not yet, love, it's Bonny's turn." Quarrel and anger had been so frequent between the two cats that, after a particularly nasty fight when both cats had paid visits to different (naturally) vets, Mr. Shardloes with all the skill and diplomacy for which *The Times*' correspondents are famous, suggested that the cats should go out in turns and that a red flag should be hoisted when Bonny was taking an airing so that Mr. Kipps could be kept at home. Francesca, although giggling, had been forced to agree. So far the system had worked, although Mr. Kipps' supporters swore that Bonny cheated on time and had much longer out roaming than Mr. Kipps.

Joanna took Mr. Kipps down to the deep basement kitchen where Francesca worked, complaining that she was like a pit pony. ('I shall start growing mushrooms soon.') The door to the game cupboard stood open, and it was only too clear that Mr. Kipps had helped himself. Joanna's shoulders sagged. It seemed the last straw. She knew from experience that Mr. Kipps took stealings into no account! They were extras pure and simple, and his normal lunch was still required as usual. She avoided meeting his eyes, poured him a saucer of milk and fled back up the stairs. But it was no use, and she knew he would be up nagging before she got to the door of her flat.

Joanna really only had the one large room, and although she could easily have afforded more and would gladly have done so, Francesca, who often took a strict Puritan line on comfort, thought one room quite enough for a girl on her own and would not lease her more.

Back in the hall again she remembered that she had not finished reading Mrs. Scobie's note. She dragged it from her pocket. After the comment about the laundry and a crossed out comment on the laundry driver's manners, there was one sentence. *"Your friend is waiting upstairs for you. I thought that was all right."*

Joanna rushed upstairs. Ted. It could only be Ted.

She could see the door to her room swing open.

A girl came to the door of the room and stared at her. She was taller than Joanna, a large, fair, sumptuous creature whom Joanna at once recognised. Sybil. She was an art student, a pupil of Ted's who also occasionally acted as model in the life class.

Joanna halted in disappointment and dismay.

Sybil gave a tentative smile. She was nervous of Joanna whom she regarded, not without reason, as clever, aloof and forbidding. She also admired her appearance, which would have startled the farouche Joanna, and deeply envied her for having such a wonderful mother with such a wonderful trade. She was also a little resentful of her. No one ought to be as assured as that.

Joanna, looking more falsely aloof and assured than ever in her disappointment, heard herself say, "Good morning," in a cold voice. She then tried to warm things up by saying hurriedly "Do come in and sit down."

"I was," said the girl.

"I'm sorry I was out. You've been waiting?"

"I had to."

Joanna, who didn't like being towered over by a woman and very rarely was, sat down.

"It's about Ted."

A lump tilted into Joanna's throat and she was surprised, and disappointed, to find it composed of pure jealousy. "What about Ted?"

Sybil nodded. A little wave of hostility flickered backwards and forwards between them. Joanna could hear Mr. Kipps' voice shouting angrily from the well of the stairs. Then the hostility faded before the genuine worry in Sybil's face. "I read the newspapers this morning, see? They found a body in Ted's flat, didn't they? I'm not saying it's anything to do with Ted, well, it couldn't be, could it? He wouldn't hurt a fly."

"I've seen him hurt several," said Joanna dryly. It was the wrong sort of joke in the wrong sort of circumstances to make to Sibyl. She stared open-mouthed. It spoiled her looks and made her lumpish. Joanna was ashamed of herself for being able to think this.

"I just wondered what I ought to do," worried Sybil. She was plainly a girl who had to do all her thinking aloud. "You see, I wonder if it's the woman I saw?"

Joanna noticed that she was trembling. She touched her hand, it was icy cold.

"I was just going to have lunch," she said gently. "Have you had any? Well, have some with me."

She made coffee, hot and very strong, thinking wistfully of Gene with whom she must next get in touch (poor Gene, it would be a very bad day indeed) and produced some cheese and toast. The two girls sat by the table and drank.

"I think it must have been the woman I saw," said Sybil, who was feeling better now.

"What was she like?"

"Well, she was *old*," said Sybil, "over forty (Sybil was not quite twenty) and she had a nice face, but funny somehow, and I remember she was standing there."

"What was she wearing?"

Sybil avoided her eyes. "Dress. Red and sort of silver. Nice." Then she said abruptly. "You've got one like it."

Joanna said nothing.

"And what's more she was watching another old thing try to push a packet of detergent through the door. I thought, 'My, you are a funny one, to watch the old thing like that and not help her.'"

So there *had* been a meeting between Miss Mouse and this mysterious woman.

"I don't suppose I'd have noticed particularly," admitted Sybil, "I never do see things much, mother says I'm in a dream half the time, but it was Ted's studio, you see... And then the old thing was carrying on so."

"What?" This was new.

"She started banging on the door," said Sybil, obviously intent now on the scene she was describing. "You know Ted's door has a brass knocker like an elephant's head that we made for him down at the school and she was using that quite quietly at first. She stood there lifting the knocker and letting it fall and talking."

She added reflectively, "I don't think she was angry though. Just puzzled and disappointed."

Sybil considered the scene for a moment. "And then she went away. She was crying, I think."

"And the other woman didn't open the door?"

"She'd disappeared. Gone into the back of the room I suppose. You can't see into it very clearly. That room's got depth. She must have heard the racket though. *Must* have."

Joanna had another thought. "Didn't anyone else in St. Ebbe's Vale notice?"

"Well, you're sort of cut off at that end, aren't you? Mrs. Brodie was sitting in her window like she always is. I waved. She knows me of course. She didn't wave back. I think she was asleep, I think she does sleep quite a bit of the day, but she doesn't like you to know it."

"Yes. That's very likely," said Joanna. She thought about the implications of this story. It had always been on the cards that Mrs. Brodie had missed a sight of the mysterious woman. She didn't think it changed anything there. But what about Miss Brown?

"You're pretty fond of Ted, aren't you?" she asked Sybil.

Sybil nodded. "He treats me like I'm someone. As though he actually *liked* me."

"I should think lots of men like you, Sybil."

"Yes. And I know what for," said Sybil. She sighed.

"I think it would be best if we don't talk about this."

"All right," agreed Sybil, getting up. " If you say so."

"Not just for the moment anyway. We'll have to talk about it later. But leave things for the police first."

"Suits me," said Sybil. "And anyway," she went on, relaxed and happier now, "it's best to leave it for old Ted isn't it? I'm sure he'll explain it all to the police."

"I expect so," said Joanna. "I expect so." But after Sybil had gone she totted up her thoughts. Joanna had always realised Miss Brown was lying the second time and telling the truth the first time.

She had seen her supposed friend and although she had not succeeded in talking to her she had not been angry, she had gone away 'puzzled and disappointed'. She had tried again, and this time had met Ted and Joanna and once again been disappointed but still not angry. Nor had she been angry when she met Joanna that day in Lyons. However there had been a *second* meeting with the woman, and it was this interview which had made Miss Brown cry in anger 'She has been dead ten years' and 'I didn't see her', 'I made a mistake'.

"Dead ten years," Miss Brown had said. "I did not see her." But the woman had had her interview with Miss Brown all right. In a way it was the reason she had died. She had done her best to avoid the interview (everyone is entitled to their privacy), but it had taken place.

When she first saw Little Brown Mouse at the door, she had been first surprised, then horrified, then fatalistic. Life had hitherto separated them but if it now insisted on reuniting them she would have to accept it. She had listened to the tapping on the door with ironic humour. She stood at the back of the room among Ted's paints and brushes and canvases and listened to Miss Brown knock. 'Hoity toity, Miss Mouse,' she thought, 'you are bold today.'

But she knew that Miss Mouse was not truly bold and never ever could be. She was however interested, passionately, keenly interested, and this could make her quite as persistent and troublesome. She remembered of old that deep interest Miss Mouse had always shown in her. She had resented it. But she had been in a position where she had to take people into her life in order to live at all. "A sort of vampire landlady," she told herself mirthlessly.

Ted's studio, as lit from the one window looking on St. Ebbe's Vale and the skylight, was a utilitarian room. Ted worked in here; now he was obliged to live here too. But he had taken no pains over it. His working area was tidy because this was how Ted preferred it to be and his living area was squalid because this was how it happened to be at this particular moment. If Joanna came in, or his cleaning woman (once a week for an hour), or Ted took the fit, it would be cleaned up.

All fell silent. The hammering ceased and after a second the woman in Ted's studio crept to the window. She looked out. Her eyes met the direct gaze of Miss Martin Brown's full on. Impossible now to pretend. They had met face to face. She saw Miss Martin Brown's face show recognition, pleasure, satisfaction and hope. She saw those thin nervous features on which the years since they had last met had made their mark. She saw the lips droop and sag as she retreated from the window and Miss Martin Brown knew she was not going to get in *that* time.

"Once a neurotic, always a neurotic," she said to herself. And then, "She will know me again."

They met, as the Fates were arranging things for their own good joke and not for Miss Martin Brown or the woman, for the second time several days later in Cornmarket. They might not have met for weeks or years, for in the past there had been no collision, but they met again at the corner by the clock and as the bells of Oxford chimed midday they saw each other again.

Miss Martin Brown's face expressed surprise, then bewilderment, then embarrassment. But she did not pretend for one moment she had not recognised, such subtlety was not for her. She was even just a little bit angry. Her former friend accepted all this mixture of emotions. She had done her best to see that she was not offered this particular plateful but what must be must be. Then she detected a shadow of satisfaction on Miss Brown's face, as though she had done something clever. 'Why, she's actually been *looking* for me,' she thought resentfully.

She beckoned.

So she had her interview with Miss Mouse. In a way it was the reason she died.

Chapter 7

The Evening

THE EVENING was having a meeting about Joanna—that is to say two members of it were: her Uncle the Ambassador and *The Times'* correspondent, retired. They were talking in worried tones about the murder about which, since they were old wise, worldly men they knew and guessed much more than Joanna did.

"Frankly, I'm worried about the girl," said her uncle, Sir Joseph. "I feel responsible. Damn it, I am responsible. What with her father in Scandinavia arbitrating how many herring can breed in the North Sea and her mother out looking at the faces of a tribe of Head Hunters in New Guinea (and God knows what my own wife is going to look like this autumn in consequence) there is no one but me. Except me mother in Donegal and praise be *she'll* never get to hear of it." His old mother was the terror of the family.

The Times' correspondent tapped his teeth with

all the suavity and aplomb associated with the great newspaper he had so long worked for. "Nasty business," he said. Originality had never, after all, been expected of him.

"It'll be in the newspapers. Falls hardly on a girl to be mentioned in the newspapers."

"You've been mentioned in the newspapers often enough, old fellow."

"Different for a marriageable young girl. And Joanna's innocent, for all her medicine."

"Very difficult."

"Quietly married and put away," said Sir Joseph wistfully, thinking back to the Hungary and Imperial Russia of his youth when a girl touched by gossip and scandal could be quietly and comfortably married and sent away on a marriage tour with her husband and off her relations' minds. "You couldn't do that with Joanna. She wouldn't go in the first place and where to in the second?"

"Charlie would be the most use," said Mr. Shardloes stroking his cat. "Notice taken of him, you know. But he's in London, one of his days."

Charlie was Lord Charleton, the great Foreign Secretary of a now unseated government. Dry, wrinkled, remote, he had been Chancellor, Foreign Secretary, Viceroy of an abandoned realm. He was living in Oxford at one of his colleges for two or three days a week, but he was a good deal in London; he still had one foot in the great world. He was old, he was deaf, he was irascible, but the glamour still hung about him. Sir Joe, although he would never have admitted it, was faintly jealous of him. "Then Balmoral. Always goes in August. Hates shooting, can't bear Scotland, always goes, can't get him back from there."

"Well, you can see why," said Sir Joseph crossly. "But Charlie never *was* there when you wanted him. Ask the Turks, ask the French, ask the Americans."

"He's always very fond of Joanna." Lord Charleton, however remote and aloof he might be to contemporaries, and he could be very snubbing indeed, was always delightful to young people as if he sensed that judgement would come from the new generations and that he still had time to win their support. For it was true that Lord Charleton was not always kindly judged by his own age group and possibly the truest verdict would come from the young ones he wooed. Or perhaps he just felt easier with the young who were in no sense his competitors. For he had competed ardently, fiercely, with the passion that had he been happily married might have spent itself in human relationships. It was natural enough that between him and Sir Joe there should be tension as well as affection.

"Very fond," said Mr. Shardloes. He was not of the social consequence of the others. He had never been a great man. But he was lively and happy keeping cats in his backyard. And he was charmingly gay and alert and had still the gift of being always on the spot when anything important happened, and this presumably was what *The Times* had paid him for.

Now he amused himself with drafting and re-drafting the obituaries of his more famous friends. He wondered sometimes if they knew that they would be sped with a judgement from his pen. 'At least it will be in good English,' he thought. "And Joanna is fond of him," he said aloud.

"What damn fools we were not to see what was brewing up..." their eyes met.

Joanna had forgotten the heat and stuffiness of an Oxford August. She sat down for a moment by the window and a drowsiness came over her gently. Mr. Kipps crawled into her lap and both their eyes closed. Her head relaxed against the kitchen wall, Joanna looked young and very tired. Mr. Kipps looked prosperous and self-contained as usual, even in sleep cats never lose their self-possession and always keep their dignity.

She stirred uneasily in her doze, thinking, but surely mistakenly, that she heard her name. Mr. Kipps jumped alertly from her lap and stared down from the window. He growled in the back of his throat, detecting the tones of an old enemy.

"Do you think she knows, or will ever guess?" said the old Ambassador sadly, "that she is herself the motive and the mainspring for the death?" He doubted it: the young are so very innocent.

Joanna, rising sourly from her sleep in that mood of depression and self-pity that arises from midday sleep in an Oxford August, heard a bell ring through the deserted house.

After a while she realised it was the telephone from the hall. Brushing her hair back she went up the three flights of dark brown carpeted stairs to the telephone. It could be Ted. She prepared for it to be Ted.

She heard a quiet official voice asking if she would talk to Inspector Pinching on the telephone. Then she heard a deeper voice, but still quiet and official, and with a pronounced Oxfordshire accent, ask her if she would mind visiting him at the police station. "I thought you'd rather come down like this, miss," he said with great politeness, or even kindness.

When she got there everyone was still polite but there was another quality to their politeness. They seemed, she thought, a little sad with her.

Inspector Pinching, who was waiting politely at the door of his office for her just as if she was a royal visitor, showed himself to be a middle-aged man with a pink face and very clean hands. He reminded Joanna of one of the surgeons she had studied under. Inspector Pinching shook hands and said he had once met her father.

"Oh yes," said Joanna cautiously. "Where was that?"

"Assizes. He was defending a man."

"Oh yes. He doesn't do so much criminal work now."

93

"No, well he's too big a man now, isn't he?" said Pinching in a friendly fashion.

"And what happened to your man at the Oxford Assizes?"

"We got a conviction," said Pinching with satisfaction; he grinned. Joanna knew that his big success at the Assizes had disposed him well to her. She must turn this to good account for Ted.

But to her surprise they asked her very little about Ted. If she knew where he was and so on. But they accepted her answers. They were so careful with her it hurt.

The police had discussed Joanna before she even arrived.

"Get it out of her plain. No argie-bargie!" One had said.

"We've got to be careful. She's protected three deep." Pinching spoke.

A look passed between them.

"We can't ask her to identify the body unless we are reasonably sure she *could* do it," said Pinching. "Anyway"—with a changed manner—"it's not something I'd like to ask any young girl to do."

"She's a doctor," said the other one stoutly; he was not imaginative himself.

"She's not usually asked to look at a body in these particular circumstances"—the word came oddly to him—"circumstances," he said again. "What a word, eh? I'm not a prude and any police officer sees plenty of the worst side of things, but this gets me. I think it's the waste. All that love, affection and talent turning destructive, burning into itself—" he broke off the sentence.

"Remember we don't know for sure," said his colleague prosaically.

"People who are going to murder very rarely announce it in advance," said Pinching suddenly, as if this was something he had to say.

"Unless they're loopy," observed the other.

"And then we don't believe them. We don't believe them."

Finally he asked if she would mind looking at something.

Joanna drew back, although it was absurd that she, who knew so much about bodies, should shrink from this one.

"No, not the body," he said quickly. "Of course not. A trunk."

It was a big trunk. *The* trunk as Joanna at once understood.

"Have you ever seen it before? Do you recognise it." Joanna looked at the trunk, she knew that black shape, she knew the kick on the side, where she had fallen over and been lamed for a week, that stain which was wine, she knew the initials.

She raised her head. "Before I say anything will you tell me one thing. Do you suppose I know the woman who was found in the trunk?"

He was silent. Then he answered her obliquely. "That is not a question I propose to put to you now. But I hope you will answer mine."

Joanna looked at the initials F.R.C. Francesca Rose Chinnery.

"Yes, I know this trunk, I've seen it often enough. It belongs to Mrs. Armour. My landlady.

"She was born Chinnery. She had it as a girl. She's Armour now."

The policeman drew a long breath.

Chapter 8

The Second Triangle

THERE WAS A TRIANGULAR relationship (always the most difficult to handle) between Francesca, Ted and Gene. Joanna herself was conscious of it, and found herself on the edge, not quite making a quadrangle, but almost. To each one she was individually more important than any of the others but together there was a bond, a link, which she only half apprehended.

What was it made of? Perhaps it wasn't even liking, Joanna was never quite sure. Possibly it was just interests in common. They had a knowledge and understanding of art which Joanna certainly did not possess. Francesca had always backed Ted as an artist, which had made her retreat in his crisis this summer all the more remarkable. They all spoke German. They all had blue eyes. It seemed a silly list of things in common. And there must be a lot more. It was as if they had had a common experience, something perhaps which they hadn't much enjoyed, but which had marked them as companions, just as fellow passengers in a railway accident, survivors of an air crash, or sailors on a raft would feel a bond. Not, as she had said before, a bond of liking, but a link.

Francesca and Ted and Gene. Why, they hadn't met eighteen months ago; she herself, the go-between, had introduced them all. She knew so much about them yet apparently so little. She knew all about Gene's tastes and so little about his life. She knew so much about Francesca's life, and yet so little about her tastes. (She had had a sharp reminder of that not so long ago.) As for Ted he was as much a mystery as any man with whom she had been in love.

Francesca rated as an older person in Joanna's life. She was a friend of her mother, not strictly a contemporary, but bridging the gap between them. Joanna had been her child bridesmaid, she looked up to her and admired her and trusted her.

So Joanna knew, or thought she knew, all about Francesca's life; about her children who were so nearly grown up; about her husband, who had died, almost absent-mindedly, so Francesca implied, when with a little more energy he could perfectly well have lived. But although she knew Francesca was often cross and at odds with life, sometimes apparently deeply unhappy, she did not really know why.

She found herself remembering the day not long ago, only a few weeks, when she had come home to find the whole house full of smoke and the smell of burning cloth and Francesca crying at the burns on her arms. Joanna was just in time to see a last flame flare up from the stove and then die away. A few rotten black rags of fabric were in the hearth. It looked like shreds from a silk dress. "What were you doing, Francesca?" she had asked as she competently and gently dressed the burns. "Some old clothes." Francesca pushed the hair away from her face. "Some old clothes that I didn't want around," she said almost sullenly. There the matter had rested. But the next day she had heard Ted exclaiming: "Francesca, you are hopeless; I needed those clothes. I wanted them." Francesca answered but she didn't hear.

She told Gene about the incident later. He shrugged. "You know what fire means? Fire is a symbol, a substitute."

"She burnt herself pretty badly on a symbol, then," said Joanna tartly.

"Burns, ah yes, she was punishing herself." He added, "What was it she burnt?"

Joanna shrugged. "Not sure. Old painting clothes of Ted's, I think."

She was wretched and miserable at the quarrel between Ted and Francesca that she had heard rumbling on till late that night.

For a long moment Gene sat silent. Then he raised his head. "No," he said slowly, "I was mistaken. It was not herself that she punished."

"Punished? Why should she be punished? What crime could Francesca commit?" said Joanna, thinking of Francesca's innocent, hardworking life.

"Ah yes, she *has* committed a crime, poor Francesca."

Gene's rounded, child-like face was sad. "There is always a crime one has committed. But we need not expect Francesca to know the *right* one," he added half ironically, half amused.

"I find you so exasperating sometimes," said Joanna coldly.

But recalling the incident Joanna knew that Gene had been cruelly hurt and was bitterly angry.

Francesca had other friends beside Joanna. Lady Duffy, Joanna's formidable aunt, wife to Sir Joe, was intermittently a very close friend of Francesca, even though she was so much older. Joanna had no intention of encountering her alarming aunt but of seeking out her cousin Grizel who had left home in favour of a rather seedy basement flat in St. Ebbe's not far from the Vale. Grizel was known, to Joanna and Ted, as 'the beautiful moron'—she was beautiful but far from moronic, although her dreamy detached appearance allowed you to think that if you wished.

On the doorstep, going out, she met her old friend Father Mahoney. They smiled but did not speak. Father Mahoney looked depressed.

Father Mahoney hesitated for a moment and then glanced back at Joanna as if he wanted to speak to her but she had rushed on and all he saw was her back. He shook his head thoughtfully and walked on.

Grizel was on the floor cutting out the silk of a dress. She was able to sew her own clothes beautifully, which was one source of argument with her mother, who would have liked her to have excelled at something more spiritual. Grizel looked up from the floor and gave her cousin an affectionate hug. "Have you seen Mamma? Perhaps you've come from her? I'm in hiding from her at the moment."

"Oh Grizel, why?"

Grizel shrugged and picked up the scissors again. "My soul," she said. "I think the real trouble is that Father Mahoney thinks she's not an intellectual. She can't stand that, naturally."

Grizel was in the process of getting converted and was receiving tuition from Father Mahoney. Joanna sometimes thought that Grizel was moved by motives of social importance in seeking conversion, her boy friend was a member of an old Catholic family and she suspected that Father Mahoney sometimes thought this too. Well, she couldn't blame Grizel, for the young man was blond and beautiful and was undoubtedly going to be somebody. Perhaps John Saville was quite as good a reason as any other. And Grizel would certainly be wholehearted, she was that sort of girl.

"How are your babies?" she added.

"Much as usual," said Joanna sadly. "They're

mostly dead, poor little things, before I ever see them. Sometimes I see the mothers. I don't like that. Something terrible about seeing a woman in a crowd and thinking 'I know exactly what killed your baby and I couldn't do a thing about it.'"

"Oh, I do agree," said Grizel warmly. "I can't think of a thing more frightful than having a baby and then its dying. Supposing it happened to me and John?" Her eyes grew dark.

"It won't," said Joanna affectionately. "The Gods look after you. You've got the right sort of God, I suppose."

"You shouldn't say that sort of thing," said Grizel a little severely, going back to her scissors. "You need more faith yourself."

Joanna sat down and took a cigarette from the box on the table. "I've certainly got trouble," she observed. "Did you see the papers? Did you know it may be Francesca?"

"Françoise?" said Grizel absently and questioningly. She was cutting out brocade rapidly as she spoke.

"Françoise?" she repeated.

It was one of her affectations to speak French sometimes, in mocking imitation of her mother, Lady Duffy. That lady had been *en poste* in France and been much impressed; she would have liked a daughter who resembled *une fille bien élevée*, dressed impeccably (for she had once lived in the grand manner herself) or at any rate to look as if she did, and there was no denying that Grizel's clothes, although charming, did not look *haute couture* and often fell apart at the seams. She wanted a daughter scented by the Fleur de Rocaille de Caron (as used by the French nobility of the *ancien régime* and none of this Napoleonic or Louis Phillipe nonsense) and with the air of never having been to a party wilder than a *bal blanc*. What she had got in fact was a daughter, slightly *rangée* (for Grizel had got about), leggy and with a decided taste for splash in clothes.

"Françoise?" Grizel said again. She was hacking away at the brocade as she spoke. "Only way to do this is to *plunge*. Anyway I can always have a nightie out of it…" she giggled. "That will be high living, bit scratchy though…" Then she saw Joanna's face and said, "Francesca?" She stood up, picked up the local paper and read the front page. "Oh my God."

"Yes," said Joanna grimly. "You and your God. Do you have any idea where Francesca is supposed to be so we could check?"

"No. Not the slightest. Mother would know though." The bounce was knocked out of Grizel and she was serious. She picked up the paper again. "How could it be Francesca?"

Joanna noted that she carefully avoided all reference to Ted and his studio. Grizel said: "Francesca has been terribly overwrought for months. Lost a lot of weight. I took in all her skirts."

Joanna looked up at that. A thought stirred in her mind and then went away before it had properly formulated.

"And you know," said Grizel, "there was

something odd. She made her will before she went away. I know. She left it with mother."

Lady Duffy was shopping when her niece found her. She was happily turning over the goods in the large store that forms part of the Cornmarket. "Astonishing quality they have here," she said as she saw her niece. "Look at this nylon. I was here the other day buying knickers with the Duchess. She always buys her knickers here. It's the only place you can get a real bloomer."

Lady Duffy dearly loved a duchess, and she usually had one or two on her list. They were very rarely quite absolutely genuine, but foreign or very divorcée. "Of course I don't shop here *myself.*"

For the first time she seemed aware that the appearance of her niece here was strange. She smiled at her. She had taught herself a smile that was not a smile, a curving of the features in formalised benediction that did not really alter the expression at all. A beautiful woman on whom life had made many social and emotional demands (Sir Joe being far from all that was absolutely desirable in a husband), she had bitterly resented his talkative infidelities, and so *she* had withdrawn, as far as one ever *can* withdraw, into a world of her own.

"Did you want me, my dear? How did you know where I was?" She usually followed one question with another.

"Grizel told me."

Lady Duffy's expression changed slightly. "Ah yes, my little pilgrim."

"Oh, you are unkind."

"But motherly you know, my dear. I don't think her motives quite impeccable, do you?"

Joanna shrugged.

"No. I don't think I'll take these," went on Lady Duffy, putting down the knickers and smiling at the assistant. "Come away, my dear, we'll shop some other time."

She picked up a bright blue and yellow brassiere, stared at it and put it down saying, "People are extraordinary. Do you know I sat next to a woman at dinner yesterday and I made a joke about her grand-child (well, her daughter's nearly fifty and the *third* marriage)—*'enfant du miracle'*, I said and she didn't know what I meant."

"I suppose there are *some* people who've never heard of the Duc de Berry," said Joanna.

"I'm glad to see you are not one of them," said her aunt placidly.

"I want to see you about Francesca. I want her holiday address."

Lady Duffy hummed. They were passing the fruit counter, she dug a sharp finger into a grapefruit.

"Dry," she said. "Half-a-dozen," she said to the assistant.

"Do you know it?" asked Joanna insistently.

"Oh yes," said Lady Duffy, but not as if she meant to pass it on.

Joanna tightened her lips. Years of practice had

brought Lady Duffy's obstructiveness to a fine art. She knew so well how Grizel felt about her mother.

Then she looked and saw that the thin hands were gripping their bundles too tightly.

"Let me tell you," said her aunt. "None of you understood Francesca properly. She's not easy to understand. Poor Francesca, she's had to suppress *so* much of herself. In the end, when you do that, the whole system gets out of kilter. The suppressed part pushes out until it *protrudes*." The way she put it the process sounded ugly.

"You love her, don't you?" said Joanna. "I never realised that."

"She's not at her holiday address," said Lady Duffy in a cold clear voice. "I telephoned myself and spoke to Madame. She's not there and never has been there."

Joanna was silent. She had an idea there was more to come.

"There's something more," her aunt gripped her wrist. "She's not there and *never been expected*.

"But of one thing I *am* sure," she cried. "The woman in the trunk is no one we know, no one we ever knew."

So there she was, a silent, dead, unknown woman in her leather tomb.

"I don't know her," Ted had sworn to Miss Brown. The woman understood Ted would deny all knowledge. It was a fixed, determined part of their relationship. He could say nothing else. Yet he knew her, knew her better than anyone else in the world. Or so she had wished to believe. But this was because she turned towards him the face by which she wished to be known, the only one which she acknowledged—the rest of her personality, which she wished to forget, went unrecognised. And being unrecognised, could almost be said not to exist. "I think, therefore I am," said Descartes and with this view of life she wholeheartedly concurred. She had taken thought and lo, here she was.

But however you look at it, to be denied when you love, as she was by Ted, is a little betrayal, and each time there was a genuine loss, the blood of the personality seeping quietly away; she was less of a person now than she had been a year ago, than she had been six months ago. As a person she had once had a certain panache. Cavalier. Gay. But society had a special way of discouraging such people, it makes them feel foolish, gives them the laugh. There was still a lot of *élan* left but it was beginning to be, emotionally speaking, spread thin on the ground.

No one knew this better than she did herself. There was a way out.

Pre-digested, pre-fabricated, a part of her was ready to be sloughed off like a dead skin. There would be a momentary sensation and then it would be all over. She had done it before.

"No, you don't know me," she would be able to say to Ted. "Not now, not this time, not this way."

Joanna returned to her work at the hospital. The
passage of time had not been long. People were still
away at lunch. She herself felt as though aeons of
time had passed. It was high full day in the heat of
summer; the summer mists of Oxford had come
down in the sky and everywhere it was mistily grey
and sticky hot.

She sat at her desk to survey the latest batch
of letters and reports; no one who is not a
professional doctor would guess how much of
her work was done by the written word; she
consulted the reports and tests of her colleagues,
she read learned journals and the reports on
learned conferences (very rarely did she herself
attend such a conference—they were always held
in far flung capitals such as Helsinki or Sydney
and she never had the money). She gathered her
post together gloomily; there seemed only too
much written on the virus diseases of the newly-
born; pity, then, it seemed so little effective.

"Father Mahoney was in here asking for you,"
said the hospital almoner, sweeping past and out.

"He was? Why?"

The almoner shrugged. "How should I know?"
She disappeared, she was always in a hurry and
gave the impression that if she didn't hurry the
work of the hospital would grind slowly to a
stop. But then everyone was secretly convinced
that the work they did was just that bit more

important than anyone else's. As one new probation nurse (and therefore comparatively clear-eyed still) said: "You work so hard here that if you *didn't* think you were God's right hand you'd give up." Even Joanna, naturally humble as she was, thought that *her* babies were more important than the work that was done on adults.

Alice glanced at her unobtrusively and frowned. "You were a long time at lunch," she observed.

"Yes, wasn't I," said Joanna absently, fiddling with a microscope.

"And to crown it all I don't believe you ate any."

"No," said Joanna surprised. "No, I don't believe I did."

"Well, you're fat enough," said Alice brutally. "Get hold of Ted?"

Joanna shook her head; Alice was probably her one friend who could take even murder in her stride.

"Of course, I always thought he was mad," said Alice suddenly. "It's in his pictures. No artist with his particular force of vision is entirely sane as we see it: he isn't living quite in our world."

So even Alice, lovingly, dispassionately had condemned Ted of murder.

Joanna felt bone weary. "I love you, Ted," she said under her breath, "I love you." It seemed all she could do. Tears filled her eyes, and dribbled gently down her nose. Her total appearance was such as would have made Mrs. Duffy weep. 'A good hearty cry would do me worlds of good,' thought

Joanna, 'and all I can squeeze out is a few miserable tears.' She felt ashamed and deeply unhappy. In her heart she too was drawing up a verdict against Ted. The signs seemed so clear. He was deeply neurotic, as the happenings of the early summer demonstrated; he had quarrelled with Francesca, there were odd tensions between them, witness the burning of the dress. Joanna told herself that Francesca had known more than she knew about Ted, had perhaps known too much.

She sat staring in front of her until Alice touched her shoulder. Then she turned to stare. Alice had a folder of papers and photographs in her hand; it was the usual sort of stiff blue cardboard folder that was used all over the hospital to file notes and documents; judging by its battered state this one had had a busy life.

"If that's more work," she said, "I've got all I want."

"Don't be a fool; I got this by bribery and corruption. Well, more bribery than corruption actually," said Alice. "I stood there for hours while Miss Pilcher described her symptoms to me and her mother's identical, but still interesting symptoms, and then her sister's absolutely fascinating symptoms. Why are people who work in hospitals always so madly neurotic? Catching, I suppose." Alice very often answered her own questions.

Joanna took the file from her hands without waiting for her to stop speaking; it fell open in her hands as if it had often been opened at this particular spot.

"Is this someone's confidential file? Ought I to look?" asked Joanna, belatedly scrupulous.

"Oh, go on," said Alice, sitting down and lighting a cigarette. "After I sweated blood for it. Besides, confidential, some of those girls down there seem to think they're editing a True-Story magazine; names they may keep quiet but nothing else. They could hardly wait, this time, to tell me."

Joanna bent her head over the papers. Alice smoked and looked at her.

"Mind you," went on Alice, "I'm not saying we should have this."

It was a file of papers from the psychiatric clinic, known as the Digby Ward; it was a file containing many names and many cases. And it was stamped DUPLICATE.

"Case histories of all the patients with violent propensities resident in the Oxford area; the police have one copy, we have this one, and there's a third up at the Ninefield Hospital... I just thought we might find someone there who had the trick of killing girls and shutting them up in cases." Anything really, she thought to herself, to stop Joanna looking like that.

"And suppose we turn up the name of our best friend?" said Joanna, looking at the file with loathing.

"Won't that be better than not knowing?" said Alice levelly.

Joanna went through the file slowly and methodically; she recognised a few of the addresses but none of the names, they were unknown figures to her, moving through the cardboard world of their madnesses. After some of the case histories she saw a line had been drawn, indicating, she guessed, that they were either dead or permanently in hospital.

She saw there were two types of figure there; there were those in whom madness was related to a physical and bodily disorder, the alcoholic, the tumour-ridden, in whose brains the blood was circulating slower and slower, even more restricted, so that they were as surely turned away from the world by their disabilities as if they were deaf or blind. The second group's madness was psychological in origin, although related possibly to some physical maladjustment; the second group was the larger. Here were the disorders of the imagination, the depressive who turned to suicide, the maniac with homicidal urges; the schizophrenic with his passing passions, and the fixed stable, terrible world of paranoia. Here was the woman who cried that she could no longer live with herself, the man who said: "When I got the urge to kill, I gotta kill; I hate myself but I got to do it"; the woman who thought she was really a man, the man who longed to be a woman, the daughter who hated her mother, the mother who hated her children.

Joanna read it, tried to understand, and thought

112

she found nothing there germane to her purpose. But when she finished the file and closed it she had, unknown to herself, read the case history of the dead woman.

"Nothing there," she said tapping with her fingers on the table. "It's only negative evidence at best," she said drearily. "If only I could get hold of Ted, he'd blow this up straight away. Why can't he come to me? He could trust me."

"Maybe it's better you don't see Ted," said Alice thoughtfully. "He may be hiding from you deliberately, if he has any feeling for you—I expect he has."

"I don't need to be protected," said Joanna angrily. "I'm adult; I can look after myself."

"There are some things everyone is better protected from," said Alice sternly; "and it may well be you are the last person who could help Ted. I don't think you've quite seen the significance of this murder. It's pretty obviously a sexual crime; Francesca, if it was Francesca in the trunk, may only be a substitute."

Joanna stared at her.

"Are you telling me?" she said slowly, "that I ought to be frightened of Ted?"

Alice looked at her very very sadly. "It's on the cards, Joanna; let's face it."

Joanna who had borne bravely the thought that Ted was a neurotic (but after all he was an artist), and that he had murdered, was asked now to face the fact that the man she had hoped to marry, by

113

whom she had hoped to have children, might be ready to kill her.

Just about this time a garbled rumour began to circulate Oxford, reaching the hospital, and eventually coming to Joanna; there had been a police statement, it was said.

"It is now believed that Mr. Ted Roman, in whose studio the body of a woman was found in a trunk, is himself dead."

This was not exactly the truth of what the police believed, but it was very near it. It was a magnificent, terrifying *coup de théâtre.*

Chapter 9

Joanna Suffers

THE BELL FROM Keble College was just audible to Joanna at three-thirty on that hot summer afternoon; she stared from her window at the Oxford scene; her laboratory was high up the building and she could look if she wished, down both the Woodstock Road and Walton Street.

It is always left to the best friend to deal the death blow and Alice had performed this traditional function unerringly; Joanna wondered if she would ever feel the same person again. Do you ever recover, pick up, face love and loving again when you have been the focus and source of death? Can you ever love straight again when you have loved crooked?

For a moment all was still and quiet but she knew that soon now the storm would burst upon her. Her distinguished father would arrive from London, her mother (who, whatever her aesthetic drawbacks, was a devoted mother) would come pelting back from Borneo or the Himalayas, complaining bitterly about public transport, and overwhelming her daughter with the trinkets and toys she had brought from abroad. At heart she still thought of her serious hardworking Joanna as a toothy little girl of ten, perhaps because hers was the one face she had rarely been allowed to get her hands on. Mother had never been undividedly in favour of Ted, although admiring his work, regarding him, perhaps with justice, as too dangerous a plaything for her little girl.

"He's very adult," she had said to Joanna after their first and indeed only meeting.

"What of it? So am I," said Joanna, a little irritated.

"You seem very serious, very intent," said her mother gravely. "I'm not at all sure it's the same thing. In fact, it isn't." And then seeing that she had really wounded her daughter. "Oh, Joanna, you're a bearer and a sufferer but not really a doer; and I think that's what you need to be with Ted."

"I don't see why."

"Because," she added, "like all artists, he is a little mad."

"That doesn't matter," said Joanna. "I'm sane enough for us both."

"Oh I grant you," said her mother, irritated in her turn. "The *unshakeable* sanity of you and your father, it's the most tiresome thing about you."

116

'Well, mother was right,' thought Joanna, 'and here I am bearing and suffering.' Her life seemed to have collapsed about her; Ted, with all his bright promise, gone, Francesca perhaps murdered; only Gene was left —Gene the indestructible. "I'm tough as old boots," he used to say gaily, "hard-boiled old boots at that." But you could never really think of Gene as hard-boiled; he was too soft and gentle. There might be a top surface of toughness and charm but underneath was an affectionate person. It was not easy to assess the source of Gene's charm; it was not an obvious charm, like that of Sir Joe, direct, commanding, maddening, but quieter, more feminine, based really on liking people, on wanting to be liked. Gene, of course, had other qualities that matched with this: he was insatiably curious, always longing to know how other people lived. "Go on, tell me, what next, how did you do it?" were questions always on his lips.

Joanna had met Gene first when she was recovering, rather unsteadily and in fits and starts, from an unhappy love affair. Gene had completed the cure; he had propounded his peculiar philosophy of life, namely, one did not accept unhappiness, one adapted oneself, created a new happiness for oneself. And Joanna who had begun to believe her mother's dictum that she was a sufferer, was in the mood to accept the truth of this.

The next day she met Ted. It was inevitable, having just been in love with Mansel, a brisk, get-ahead young lawyer from Queen's, that she should turn gratefully to Ted who was relaxed, bohemian and slightly scruffy. Paradoxically, it was Mansel, who appeared a pillar of the Establishment, who was at odds with society, angrily and constantly rejecting everything, finally even Joanna, whereas Ted, who looked a very angry man, was easy going and took things as they came. Joanna had believed this to be because he was utterly confident of success on his own terms (whereas poor old nerve-ridden Mansel was not) but now she wondered if it was not because he was entirely and absolutely indifferent. Once again she told herself she had made the fundamental error of loving for the wrong reason and for what was not really there. So, angrily, Joanna reasoned, humanly if unconsciously, trying to wean herself away from the love that looked like being so costly.

It would be good to see Gene again; to him at least she could talk; there would be a spattering of psychological terms, a good many references to Freud, but anyway complete understanding. Perhaps he could help her to understand the position she was in. At the moment she was surprised to find that underneath all her emotions of misery, worry, unhappiness was a clear note of anger. She was deeply ashamed of this, although a psychologist would have told her that it was the note of life, it represented the essential Joanna striking out. It was healthy, if egotistically selfish.

Joanna, victim of her society, convicted herself of bad taste.

She recalled a conversation about Ted. It had taken place in Gene's own home. Gene lived in precise, tidy happiness in a minute flat above his office. He was house-proud. You could see this from the neat cooking shelves with pots and pans, the carpenter's bench and the electrical tools, for Gene was very practical, his embroidery frame (so good for the nerves), the rows of books: modern novels, poetry, cookery and psychology... "Do you want so much to understand other people?" she had asked once.

"No, it is rather myself; or is it the same thing? Where does self end and the other person begin? What are the limits of human personality?"

Joanna had shrugged and given the stock medical answer. "Cells, glands, genetic instructions imprinted on nucleic acids."

"Not even a bus but a tram? Oh no, Joanna, we can even change from being a bus to being a taxi."

...Yes, Gene believed in freedom in his way.

"But what makes some people bricklayers, some people doctors, like me, and some people artists like you and Ted?"

Gene had flushed with pleasure, a clear pretty pink, that Joanna oddly admired, at her comment on himself, but had spoken of Ted. "I can tell you what makes Ted an artist, what gives him his vision, and what also prevents him being a complete person."

Joanna had looked up quickly; they were the first
words of warning.

"You know this history of Ted's? Ah no, I see you
don't. When he was little, oh so little, war came to
his part of the world, you know that?"

"It came to my part of the world too," commented
Joanna dryly. "Evacuees, bombs. I remember."

"It came to Silesia in a nastier sort of way; there
was bombardment: a winter bombardment,
somehow that is always worse; Ted was little but
he remembers it. Then the enemy retreated; and
for Silesia this time there were two enemies, so two
bombardments, the attacker and the retreater. Ted's
people were not peasants, not country people, but
they left their little town for the country. There is
much forest."

Joanna looked at him uneasily.

"Ted and his mother sheltered under some trees;
it was, no doubt, a silly thing to do; but the mother
was frightened and Ted was only little, so little that
he remembers his petticoats getting wet in the
snow as he crouched." Gene added, "he was not
yet old enough, you see, to have been britched,
they still called it that and behaved so in Silesia
before the War."

Joanna frowned, "Well, he picked up his little
petticoats and then what?"

"A shell landed not far from the tree, they weren't
hurt by that, although Ted says his hearing went.
He remembers seeing and not hearing, like a

monstrous nightmare. The next shell didn't touch the tree either (they were not very good, those gunners) but it did enough damage, splintering the wood of the tree with blast and sending out great darts of steel. Ted's mother was pinned to a low branch; she was, in effect, crucified."

"Does Ted remember all this?"

Gene nodded. "And it explains his need for the dark places. Under a tree, fear of the open plains, agoraphobia, and, of course, one associated this with a *womb*-consciousness; he had lost his mother."

He looked at Joanna seriously.

She didn't know whether to laugh or cry.

She recalled this conversation, and the heat of Gene's little room as she sat looking out of the window. Did the roots of crime and the rejection of life go back so many years?

A nurse bustled in from the ground floor with a specimen which she took over to Dr. Broster in the corner; he had been waiting for it.

"Hello," she said to Joanna as she went back. She eyed her with interest, the rumours were well around now. "Work piling up?"

Joanna nodded and fiddled with the papers on her table. "How are you doing down in Neurology?"

"I'm over in Gynae now," said the nurse, "And glad I am to go; sure that was a butcher's cell!" and she raised her eyes to heaven. "They walked in and we carried them out."

Joanna did not answer directly. She knew that no one department ever had a good word for the next; it didn't mean anything.

"Anyway, in Gynae and Obstetrics there is at least hope," went on the nurse.

Joanna grunted.

"Except when we see you around, of course. We hide the babies when we see you coming. Oh, that reminds me, I was going to tell you..."

"Hi," called Dr. Broster from the other side of the room. "Come over here, will you."

Alice glared at the nurse's departing back. "Stupid woman."

"She didn't mean any harm," said Joanna drearily. "I expect it's true anyway." She turned back to her work, but the interview had somehow sharpened her. She had made up her mind to telephone the police and then she would go round to see if Gene was home. She tidied her papers.

"Mind if I use your phone?" she said to her chief, who by virtue of his position had a tiny office and a more or less private telephone of his own.

He nodded without speaking, but he looked at her intently.

She shut herself into the little cubby hole with its perpetual smell of ether and iodoform and other odours more human but less pleasant. It was in its usual disorder of papers, diagrams, charts and books; still from their disorder proceeded a regular flow of articles about prolonged unconsciousness. They were valuable, if dull, articles and Joanna knew that her chief would soon be moving on to become the head of a great medical research department in the University of London and that she would have to make up her mind whether or not she would accompany him. Up to now she had been undecided, but she had no doubts now, she would go; better leave this never-never land of false hopes for ever.

She got through straight away.

She assumed a practical and brisk voice. "I want to know if you have any definite identifications."

"Identifications?" said the voice cautiously.

"You don't have to hedge with me; you know there are two persons involved."

"How did you know that?"

"It's all over the town."

"I see." The voice was level, almost expressionless, but all the same there was in the background a faint note of stress. "Well, I'm afraid we have no news for you. You can understand that. It's only a matter of hours."

"Well, in any case that's not what I really called to say," said Joanna, summoning firmness. "I wish to identify the body."

There was a longish pause during which Joanna had time to hear the noises off; a typewriter, men's voices, someone coughing.

"I'm not a lay person in this respect, you know," she reminded them.

"That I understand; however there are circumstances..." the voice trailed away, losing for a moment its confidence.

"Do you think I don't see that?"

"I wonder if you do..." again that curious note that Joanna was too intent to notice. "Come down then, miss. Yes," the man started to sound interested. "Yes, come. You are right, it is probably an excellent idea."

Slightly sick, triumphant, panting, Joanna leaned back in the chair and put the receiver down.

Soon she would know.

She counted the cost that her knowledge would be to her and thought she could just pay it; she would pay for it in nervous energy, she would pay for it in unhappiness, she might even pay for it in a loss of power in her own work, but she must look at that face and say: "Yes, this is Francesca."

She gathered up her coat and bag and without saying anything to Alice or her chief walked out of the door, down the long staircase and into the main hospital block. Automatically she swung round by the maternity block; it was quicker.

Father Mahoney was standing quietly at the end of the corridor by the nursery and 'prems' block. He stopped Joanna as she went past. He was a strange man, not altogether easy to know, and Joanna found her feelings towards him ambivalent. She both feared and liked him. The reason she feared him was not clear to see. He was a clever man, cleverer than any man she knew except her own father. But he was simple and unpretentious; his cleverness was not the driver, but took a back seat. She found him very difficult to get hold of as a person. He wrote beautifully, but it was in the style of Cicero, or Gibbon, or Trollope. He preached very well, in the manner of Cardinal Newman. He had published two novels but they were pastiche of Dickens and Proust. It was deeply significant, perhaps, that his most valued work was a translation, in which very little of himself need directly appear; it was as if he was frightened of letting his own personality come forward, as if he must always shelter behind another and stronger form. And yet it would be mighty difficult to call him a coward. You might perhaps call him lazy. Or was it a more subtle weakness, a pride which aped humility, which would not *compete*? And was there below this a timid, loving, holy spirit? You couldn't be sure. He projected a personality that was unsympathetic and perhaps not even his own: he was a bad Press Relations Officer for himself.

"Hello," said Joanna uncertainly, her proper thoughts far away. But she wanted to be polite.

He hesitated for a moment as if about to say something else, then said "Good day."

"I'm here with Leonie Lamond to see her child," he added briefly.

"Is it ill?" asked Joanna.

"Last night the temperature went up."

"That's bad," said Joanna, with quick sympathy. "That's very bad." She was genuinely concerned; she was thinking of the smallness of the baby. "I'll go to see."

"Not now," he said gently.

"No, not now," agreed Joanna, her own troubles flooding back. "Later." ...'If there is any later,' she thought, and sighed.

He considered for a moment, weighing her need against his own; he saw that hers was the greater and wearily picked up the burden that was expected of him.

"There's some trouble? Can I help?"

Joanna withdrew: she took his help to mean only one thing.

"I don't believe, Father," she said politely. "Not anything. I mean I can't."

"It's only one way of thinking, I understand that; don't think I don't."

"It'll get me in the end though," said Joanna gloomily. The whole world at the moment seemed one vast cave of the faithful lying in wait for her.

"My dear child!" Father Mahoney was shocked and touched. "You must not talk like that."

They stared at each other: he saw the little lines leading from the corners of her forehead down to her eyes and the deeper thinner ones from mouth to nose.

"And in any case, that is not what I meant."

"Oh, there's no help you can give me," said Joanna, remembering. "But thank you for offering. Pray for me if you like."

Father Mahoney watched her back disappearing through the door, half-exasperated, half-sympathetic, wholly tender. 'Poor child,' he thought. 'Poor silly child.'

Only when she had completely disappeared did he remember that he had not asked her the question that was large in his mind and that she alone could answer. He tried to tell himself that this was in any case a question that the doctors would ask Joanna but he knew instinctively that his own intuitions had been faster to work.

Later he was to see this very lapse as a sign of grace. Someone had left a bunch of white flowers, freesias, lilac, roses, outside the ward and Joanna had been plucking distractedly at the blossom as she spoke. A little scattering of petals lay on the floor.

Chapter 10

The Oxford Police

JOANNA WENT ON FOOT. You never could get on a bus in Oxford. To get to the police station she had had to pass down the crowded streets of summer Oxford. The Cornmarket was baking in the sun of this unexpectedly hot, dry August. Joanna thought wistfully of cool Scottish moors, of trout rivers glinting in the sun, of deep Devon valleys, of the sea sweeping in wide curves round the coasts of Sussex, and here she was roasting in the heart of England, bemused with murder.

At the corner where the cross roads meet, and town and gown merge, she stood for a moment before the traffic and listened to the great bell of Christ Church toll the half hour. Christ Church's bell seems perpetually in mourning for great Wolsey who built the vast quadrangle and died before the stones were settled. Christ Church remembers its Cardinal, pretty well the only Cardinal to win fame in England before Newman caught the High

Anglican Church bathing and ran off with its cope.

Ted had once painted a picture of this spot and it hung now in the New Venture Gallery not far away. It was a successful picture. There was nothing chancy about Ted's skill as a painter, he knew what he was about and where he wanted to go and how to get there, even his failures were not of vision and were never dull, but were the result rather of having too much to say. But Christ Church in December had been a full blown success.

On a sudden impulse Joanna turned left and swung down the little passage way which would bring her to the Art Gallery: it was still roughly on her way to the police station.

There was no one about. She could see the girl who ran it talking to a young man in the little courtyard beyond; she waved and hurried on. She walked up the narrow staircase to her picture, because it was her picture, Ted had given it to her. There it was in all its flaring reds and blues. People said Oxford was grey but Ted had a better eye for colour and knew that in the shadows lurked all the gaiety of medieval Oxford. Painted in Ted's very individual style in which all colour was broken down into dashes without being in the least like the Post-Impressionists or Seurat, it had, too, the dramatic point which his pictures always had. In this case the dramatic point was a small quiet figure placed half way along a wall, not with a story to tell (Ted's pictures were not in the least anecdotal

129

or pictorial), but a place to fill, a focal point, a point of tension.

Joanna, who was perhaps in an imaginative mood, saw in this figure painted against the massed grey stone all the past of Oxford, the medieval university with its wandering scholars, disputations, learned doctors, drinking songs and taverns. And yes, too, the kindliness and the humanity; the protest of the individual against the assaults of the crowd.

She turned away from the picture sadly: the man who had painted that picture was, one way or another, dead. In this picture had been expressed a joy of living, a love of people and stones and bricks and wood, a love for the world; and yet she had to believe that the man who had painted it had been deeply implicated in murder.

Her friends saw her at the bottom of the staircase. For a moment she thought they were talking about her and then she saw that they were arguing. Mirry, the girl who ran the gallery and subsidised it out of a tiny private income, was always arguing with someone. This time it was with Kane, a young university don and one of her chief, if most tiresome supporters.

"Hello, Kane," said Joanna. Kane glared at her. It was amazing how the more austere disciplines (Kane was an economist of so abstracted a type that he dealt entirely in numbers and calculating machines and had the undivided prime written on his heart) led you to the wilder arts. Kane went for the noisier composers and played the jazz trumpet very badly. "Where's Simon?" Simon was an undergraduate, but Kane's best friend, and he was always seen with him, although usually lurking at a distance: Joanna had last seen him giggling behind a pillar at a Commem Ball while Kane led the trumpets in a steel band; she looked round for him automatically.

"In hospital," said Kane with a scowl, as if it was somehow Simon's fault he was ill. Possibly it was.

Mirry smiled, she was a kind girl and although preoccupied with painters and paintings, liked what got through of the outside world.

"He had a nasty accident," said Mirry, "fell off his bike; I've often told him he ought not to ride it." She had a slight lisp.

Simon possessed an ancient, tall, straight old bicycle that had long lost any strength and was held together with string. He was quite rich enough to afford a motorcar and indeed did possess one but the university authorities had forbidden him (as they had full powers to do) to use it in Oxford, where he was extremely accident-prone.

"Kane's *lonely*," she said.

"No I'm not," said Kane, still scowling; "I'm working. Never lonely when I'm working."

This was true.

Domestically, however, he was a chained man. His wife Laudia (named by a High Church Latinist mother) gave the orders in *that* house, which was one reason Simon kept his distance. Kane was allowed every freedom, nay encouragement in his academic labours and studies—which indeed his wife, a genuine intellectual, respected and admired—but every paragraph in print, every hour spent in discussion with friend and foe (the two strangely alike in his métier), had to be paid for by a stint in the kitchen or the nursery. Only when Laudia was in hospital having a baby, which happened with mathematical regularity, as you might expect, did Kane escape.

"How's the baby?" asked Joanna absently. She was fond of the baby who although only three had the makings in him of a juvenile delinquent and had swallowed and apparently digested his mother's engagement ring. He was obliged by his proud parents to mingle with an age group two years older than his own because his I.Q. gave him a mental age of five. As Jim still couldn't speak, I.Q. or not, this made him a very anxious little boy and accounted perhaps for the delinquency.

"Which baby?" asked Kane sourly. "Laudia and I have three."

"Well, I suppose I meant the *first* baby," said Joanna, thinking that Laudia had four, counting Kane. "He was my baby. I delivered him. The first I ever did."

"Yes," said Kane, "I remember you telling my poor Laudia that, just when she was still breathing deeply and relaxing; she nearly had hysterics."

"It went off all right."

"Yerss... but wasn't there a moment when you were *both* looking at a book on obstetrics and it was left to the probationer nurse to tell you you'd got it upside down?"

"Fancy Laudia remembering that," said Joanna, a little cross. Then she smiled. "I had a whole library outside that I meant to pop out and consult, but Laudia never gave me time."

"Good for her," said Mirry.

She had once had a passing love for Kane, but all she remembered about him now was that he was the only reliable man she had around to hang her pictures; she was full of them. "We sold *three* pictures last week, a Heffer portrait —one of the Vice-Chancellor—a lovely little Pinto landscape, all deep grey, and a very nice water colour of the Cherwell... all to tourists." She was triumphant.

"So I thought we might have a little party to celebrate."

"To cheer up Kane's loneliness?"

"I'm not lonely," muttered Kane, in a wild way.

"Why don't you and Ted come?" went on Mirry, giving him no sympathy.

There was a silence and Joanna saw in Kane's eyes that he knew or had heard about Ted: Mirry of course couldn't be expected to know about anything.

"Ted's away," she said in a strangled voice and prepared to walk away quickly.

"Is he?" Mirry sounded puzzled. "I was sure I *saw* him in Catte Street today. Well, I never, are you sure?"

But Mirry lived in a hazy world and was always
mistaken. How could it be Ted? Odd things were
always happening to her; she was like a short-
sighted person looking at a landscape; half the
things she saw were not there or were really
something else.

At the police station Big Tom had moved on and
was striking four o'clock. Four o'clock, tea time,
and all over Oxford tea-kettles were boiling and
people were making toast and eating Fuller's walnut
cake.

In the police station a large young policeman in
uniform but with a bare head was carefully carrying
two cups of tea down a corridor. He knocked at a
door and went in; the two men sitting there took
their tea and went on with their conversation.

"You've got the girl coming down?" asked the
taller and older man.

"She would come. I was all for keeping her out
of it. Then I thought, 'Why not let her come
down?'"

The older man made a gesture of distaste.

"I don't honestly know who I'm going to get to
do the identifying if I don't get her," replied
Pinching; he began to look very tired, and indeed
he had been up for what felt like days. The body
had been discovered just in time to prevent him
getting home to a dinner party arranged weeks ago
by his ambitious wife, it had prevented him getting

up to bed and at the moment he had the slightly sick feeling that some cases still gave him. You expected, surely, you expected violence, but some cases were so peculiarly pointless and tragic that even a tough policeman felt the strain. He did not intend, however, to have it go on much longer. It was going to be cleared up and settled.

There was a silence then the older man said softly:

"So that's how you're going to do it. That's how it's going to be."

Joanna found she was more nervous than she had expected. It was all very well to tell yourself that these things were a commonplace for you; if your nerves, and blood and heart denied it what could you do?

She was led into the small bare room, all this was as she expected, what she had visualised to herself. What she had not expected was that the light would be upon her, that she too would be watched, observed, identified. This felt odd.

She turned eyes towards the face; she looked for straight black hair with a tinge of grey, she looked for curving delicate features, and she saw grubby pale hair and swollen plump features. She had feared to see the face of Francesca. Perhaps deep down, in her unconscious mind, in the labyrinth which is never freely known, she had expected to see the face of Little Brown Mouse.

It was not the face of Francesca. It was not Miss Martin Brown.

She found herself looking down upon a perfectly strange face.

Joanna walked home alone in an unexpected quietness of mood; she felt released, as though the whole crime was after all nothing that touched her. This was an irrational surge of feeling let loose by relief; something she had dreaded had not after all been the case and therefore she was happy: it was a compensation for the intensity of her apprehensions.

As she walked down the High Street she passed Gene's office, above which was his little flat. She looked up. The windows of the flat were open, and there were flowers in the window box. Gene must be home.

Cheerfully she went up the long linoleumed stairs, passed the office with the notice still pinned to it CLOSED FOR THE MONTH OF AUGUST, and up to Gene's front door. It was ajar.

She pushed it further open and went in.

There was a smell of furniture cream, lightly scented with lavender, there was a smell of soap and scrubbing, there was a faint smell of new bread on the air as if someone had been baking.

"Gene," called Joanna. "Hello?"

The sound of the traffic floated in through the open window, and across the street someone was playing the piano.

Gene's sitting-room was a simple exercise in Bedemeyer, that style roughly comparable to Victorian but with more of a flourish, bolder (vulgar you might say as a purist) but certainly not lacking in character, even if not a great one. There was a sofa with writhing curves which had the air of being about to burst into active life any minute and walk off. There was a dancing table, and a three-legged stool. But it was a gay, garish, positive room and it exactly reflected Gene.

Still, in spite of the feeling of the owner having just walked through on the way to the kitchen there was no one there, and no one in the kitchen or the little bedroom.

Baffled and disappointed, like a child deprived of a treat, Joanna stumped her way back down the stairs, nearly bumping into a woman coming up them with a bucket as she did so. She knew now she was in for a bad case of glooms.

The woman turned and stared at her.

Joanna walked home, passing many friends on the way, but not noticing them because she was thinking. It was not Francesca in the trunk, but it was Francesca's trunk. Where was Francesca?

And her thoughts were sombre.

And Ted? Was it true that he too was dead? And how had he died? She had asked the police but they had given her no answer, and she had been frightened to press. She did not want to believe that Ted was gone.

She thought back to that last meeting between them and the full bitterness of what it meant seeped into her, irresistibly, like salt water into clear. Soon by osmosis the bitterness would be part of herself. They had not even said goodbye. They had met, enjoyed each other's company, been a stimulus and a joy to each other, and this was to be the end. There would be no more.

Her own personal tragedy burned into her.

And then, by the corner of Park Town where she lived, the good thing happened to her.

Although she thought she was noticing nothing, she was after all a doctor, and unconsciously registered a good deal she did not notice; but the censor in her mind went tick-tock and automatically registered things of interest. There was a child standing at the corner of the road near the new traffic lights, a boy of about ten. Joanna saw him first without taking him in, and then, as the significance trickled through to her, with surprise.

"Hello, what are you doing here?"

"Well, I was waiting to see you. That is, I was hoping to," he looked carefully up and down the road. "I couldn't wait too long or Aunty will be out."

He was a boy Ted had painted, the nephew of a neighbour; because of the portrait a friendship had grown up between him and Ted. Joanna knew she was on the outskirts but she didn't mind that, she was used to it with Ted's quick friendships... she always had to be slower.

The boy looked up at her, his round brown eyes slightly popping. He was no beauty, and perhaps if he had been Ted wouldn't have painted him. It was true about Aunty, she guarded him anxiously and nervously like a prisoner, always worrying about his welfare and wet feet.

"I wanted to see you about Ted." He always called him Ted but without familiarity; he was a polite well-schooled little boy and knew all about Aeneas, the life cycle of the frog, and William the Conqueror, and was beginning Geometry.

"Oh." Joanna was bleak.

"Yes, I'm afraid it's no good, I can't keep the appointment for our last sitting. Aunty's taking me away to Scotland. I've argued and argued," he was gloomy, "but it's no good. The sleepers are booked, and you can't waste sleeper bookings."

So he didn't know, couldn't know when you considered watch-dog Aunty, about Ted and the woman in the trunk and the rumours about Ted.

"It's all right," she said.

"But it isn't all right." He peered up at Joanna impatiently, he was a very clever boy and Aunty's treatment was already brewing up a fine woman-hater: he was destined for a brilliant academic career. "Ted wanted my picture for a special show in the autumn."

Joanna shook her head. "I didn't know." But inside she was shouting at herself 'So whatever happened was unpremeditated, chance, not planned.'

139

She looked at the boy gratefully.

It wasn't that he had passed a vote of confidence in Ted, he was too young for that and anyway he didn't know anything about the matter. But he had reminded her forcibly that Ted was a person looking hopefully to the future, that he was a real person. For a time she had been out in limbo, now she clicked back into herself again and with her own right and proper view of Ted based on her own experience of him as a person and a painter.

Grizel's words came back into her mind: "You could do with a bit more faith yourself."

"I will have faith," she said, as if that was the only thing in the world. "I will believe."

But life knew a trick worth two of that.

The houses in Park Town were gilded in the afternoon sun. It was cooler now, and the smell from the trees and the roses was sweet and enjoyable.

Francesca's house was still and peaceful, the air stuffy, like most old houses closed all day in the summer. Mr. Kipps came down the stairs, cheerfully alert and friendly, and nudging Joanna with his hard little head to let him out.

She still had the problem back on her hands. Francesca was mysteriously away, Ted was gone, and in a trunk had lain a dead woman, cosily in the Oxford summer.

And the house, which should have been empty, was filled with an alien presence.

Chapter 11

The Last Evening

SHE STOOD IN THE NARROW dark hall and everything told her that the house had been entered and was perhaps still occupied. A window had been opened and the breeze blew through, a coat hanging on the back of a door had been knocked to the floor and there was a faint smell of cigarette smoke: the smell of a Cyprus cigarette, scented and gently luxurious.

The smell of the cigarette was a clue. But she knew who had entered the house without that. It was as unmistakable to her as if he had drawn and signed 'Ted' to a picture of it happening.

She rushed forward and shouted, "Ted, Ted," but the walls of the stair pit caught her voice and smothered it and there was no answer in return.

She mounted the stairs slowly, still calling, Mr. Kipps following her behind miaouing gently. Ahead of her a thick velvet curtain billowed out. But there was no one behind it.

141

"And why should there be?" she reminded herself "Ted wouldn't *hide*."

There was no one in Francesca's big sitting-room. No one in her little book room, no one in the room Ted had once had, no one in the empty tidy rooms occupied in term-time by the girl students. No one in Joanna's own little flat right at the top.

No one. No one. No one.

She sat down on the stairs and Mr. Kipps crawled on her lap. He seemed particularly pleased with himself and purred at her in a self-satisfied way. She stroked him absently.

Then she went back through the rooms again. Looking. Searching. And this time she found traces of someone else's passage through the house. Every other room including her own had been entered. There was a drop of ash here, a smell of smoke there, and someone had rested on the bed in what had been Ted's room. There was the impression of a long solid shape on it.

Joanna put her face down by the pillow and sniffed and met a smell once loved and enjoyed by her, the peculiar mixture of soap and smoke and paint that always hung around Ted's hair. Mingled with her misery was a faint amazement. How muddle-headed of Francesca not to have sent all these things to the laundry before she went away. It emphasised how very distracted Francesca had been those last few weeks.

Mr. Kipps jumped up on the bed and started to knead it with his paws, purring loudly as he did so. It was only too clear where *he* had spent the afternoon. Even as she watched he curled up and went to sleep.

There was something alarming and chilling in this occupied silence. She remembered Alice's words of warning about Ted's love for her, and her suggestion that Ted might have a very ambivalent feeling towards Joanna.

He loved and was attracted, granted; but perhaps he was also repelled and antagonistic.

As she sat there a smell which had been there all the time in the background was strengthening itself imperceptibly minute by minute and forcing itself upon her. A smell of gas was floating upwards from the basement kitchen.

Suicide. The word formed quickly in her mind.

For a moment Joanna did nothing at all, then her training asserted itself, and getting a towel from Francesca's cupboard she damped it and draped it round her throat and mouth.

She went down the back stairs to the kitchen.

Francesca always swore there were rats in her kitchen and although both the Rodent Officer and Mr. Kipps denied this indignantly it was certainly a dark and lurking place which none of Francesca's carefully planned bright colour schemes really lightened.

Joanna expected to find Ted lying there.

But when she staggered across to the old stove to turn off the tap and throw open the window

143

she was aware that there was no one there.

Ted didn't mean this gas for himself but for me, she thought, maybe not to kill me, but anyway to stupefy me... 'Poor Ted', she thought wryly, 'he always was a damn bad handy-man: this amount of gas wouldn't make me unconscious, it would just make me sick.'

Her first impulse was to telephone the police and her second was to run straight out of the house.

She looked at the back door and saw that the key was gone.

Ted had the entry to the house.

If it *was* Ted.

Francesca's kitchen was a strange place, it reminded you that when you came down to it Francesca was very undomesticated. There was a row of empty milk bottles lined up against one wall close to the door; they were quite clean but it was clear that Francesca although she washed them regularly, forgot to put them out for the milkman. There were piles and piles of methodically laid-away, but absolutely useless boxes and containers, and layers of brown wrapping paper so old and frail you couldn't have wrapped anything in it but presumably Francesca thought you could.

At the back of the kitchen tucked away so that you saw it with difficulty was a large wooden box.

Joanna had known of its existence there for years, but what she noticed now was that it was edged noticeably further into the room, as if about to progress higher into the house.

"If I open that," said Joanna to herself, "there will be someone in it. Whether alive or dead, there will be someone in it."

Across the road in the cosy sitting-room of *The Times* correspondent, the Evening, with the exception of Lord Charleton, were assembled. They were reinforced, although through no fault of their own, by a cross Lady Duffy. This had a particularly deflating effect on Sir Joe.

"You're a couple of old women," she said. "Can't you make up your mind what you've seen and what you haven't seen?"

"I know what I've seen," said old Shardloes. "It's interpreting it that's so diffy." He dropped into Edwardian slang sometimes. It was a sign of nervousness and puzzlement.

"Deevy," jeered Lady Duffy.

"Don't pretend you didn't use that sort of slang yourself once, Milly," he said sharply. "You're old enough."

"Rubbish, of course I'm not, I doubt if my own mother used it."

"We were both here. I saw her too," said Sir Joe. "I saw her hanging round that house in St. Ebbe's Vale. I saw her, I tell you."

"You're going to have to make it clear what you were both doing there," said Lady Duffy. "The police are going to want to know that."

"Been out to the Founder's Luncheon at Holy Innocents."

"The fact that this was after a luncheon is going to be of interest."

"We weren't drunk." Sir Joe was even more sulky. "Good God, old Charleton was with us, and going moaning on about space research. We none of us had the spirit to drink. Made my blood run cold. Believe the old devil sees himself as the first Governor-General of the moon."

"He's cold-blooded enough," said Lady Duffy, who had never made any headway with Lord Charleton.

"I tell you I saw her hanging about outside the house not ten minutes ago. Of course I knew her face. There must be something... you know." Sir Joe looked anxious. "She's a tricky customer. Loopy, *I* think."

"We ought to help Joanna," said Lady Duffy, turning to stare at the house across the way.

"Now? Is she in?"

"Yes. *I saw her go in.*"

"It's all so difficult," said Lady Duffy. "I'm not protecting this woman, mind, I want to protect *Joanna*." Her face looked sad. "She's in *love*." She looked at Sir Joe. "You know, after fifty odd years I'm sick to death of love and being in love and people falling in love. It's a damned nuisance."

"There's no love about killing," said Mr. Shardloes. "Don't run into *that* sort of nonsense. Never mind what the books say. No one kills for love. There has to be good solid hate."

Joanna had a picture forming in her mind now of the woman who had been in the trunk in St. Ebbe's. She added it to what she had now seen in the mortuary.

She was older than Joanna was herself, but physically similar. She had a mental history and she had been in hospital with Miss Brown. She had an educated background. And she had the entry to Ted's studio, whether he was there or not. She wore, sometimes, a red and grey striped dress.

There was something else too about her, but this thought remained elusive in Joanna's mind.

"I can run across the road any time I like," she told herself. "There's nothing to fear."

But all the same fear was with her, eating into her through the skin, through the flesh into the bone and nerve. It was an inch of shapeless fear at first, then it took shape and formalised itself into a fear of Ted, whom she had thought dead, and must now be alive. He had been in this house and he could return. Would return, she told herself, looking at the window.

Through the basement window she saw the flick of a tabby tail and realised that Mr. Kipps had got out; she minded this defection, oddly. Kipps was no hero but he was company and he had a voice.

Her anxieties and fears gradually centred upon the box, which seemed more and more prominent in the dusky kitchen. High up on the wall the bright sunlight from outside was caught in the pool of light, but the air of the kitchen was murky.

There was a stuffy atmosphere to Francesca's kitchen, as if too many old things had been shut up there for too long. And although high upon the shelves where Francesca kept her preserves, you could see the faint ruby gleam of bottled plums, the deep yellow of apples and pears and the orange glow of marmalade this did not dissipate the impression of oddness.

She remembered what she had thought.

"If I open that trunk," she said, "there will be someone in it. Alive or dead, there will be someone in it."

"And if I don't open it," she told herself idiotically, "it will remain empty."

She opened it slowly and carefully, it was heavy but in good repair and easy enough to manage. She remembered now that Francesca used it to store the laundry in. And at first, when she opened it she thought that was just what it did contain.

A heap of old laundry.

Then she saw only a few things there: a heap of old clothes, a white petticoat, long stockings, shoes. And on top a red and grey striped dress. All neatly, politely folded and put away.

Somehow they gave the appearance of having been put carefully away against the next wearing.

For the first time it dawned on her that the woman in the red and grey dress was in some sense a mirage.

"No, no," she cried out. "You are already dead." And then as the full awfulness was borne upon her:

"If you aren't, WHO IS?"

All that hot summer day in July which was in fact to be her last on earth the woman waited in the studio. She had the entrée to the studio, had always made use of it, although it was to be doubted if Ted knew how much she was there. He knew she painted pictures there. That was the official formal reason for being there. And she paid a share of the rent. That was in the bargain. She had a right to be there.

She walked up and down, her skirts floating in the breezes she made, she didn't often wear long skirts and she enjoyed the unusual rustle. As a young woman her circumstances had not been such that silk was likely or practical for her. Indeed she had deliberately turned aside from a life that could have made them feasible for her. It was all part of the constitutional longeurs from which she suffered: and which was in itself an inherited attempt to pick up the pieces: a built-in reaction to a liability which was always probably going to be too much for her, but which her circumstances made particularly overwhelming.

Ted's studio was not a refreshing place to spend a hot summer's day. There was a stale jug of milk on the table, a plate of mortadella which did indeed look surprisingly like dead baby, a heel of old loaf and a pot of marmalade. But this was overlaid by evidence of work. A rough charcoal sketch of a horse, a spectrum of colours laid out on a palette, a ball of clay kept damp by a wet cloth. All this made it somehow an attractive place to be: it was a room in which creation could go forward.

It was, however, a room which any woman of normal instinct would have tried to clear up, and although she was not this, and had reasons of her own for not being so, she felt the pull.

She was a sturdily built woman with curling hair, and dandruff on the shoulders, not elegant, not beautiful, but a character all right, not a weakling, used to dealing with people, but quite unable to deal with herself. Beneath a surface air of composure and competence she was all at sixes and sevens: but a *nice* woman. That, unluckily, had to be admitted.

She lay back and looked at the room and thought, 'Someone ought to do something about it. I ought to do something about it.' She always enjoyed using her hands: it was pleasing and relaxing and, if carried out automatically, allowed you to be practically anonymous. But too much hard physical labour (and this she knew too) did more than make you anonymous, it wiped you out as a person. She had been wiped out once and the pieces never really got together again.

Her relationship with Ted had really been a parental one, she had hidden this carefully beneath the guise of friendship. There had been between them just that element of authority and affection and dominance that constitutes the parental relationship. Someone was always going to dominate Ted.

Of her ambivalence Ted of course knew nothing: he had no idea she was not exactly what she appeared to be.

And yet she was not mad and never lost a clear sense of her own mind and her own identity: everything she did was reasonable.

She trusted that she appeared a successful character in the world, but she feared she was also something of a comic character although not of course, to herself, *she* didn't see herself as a joke.

She knew she was a comic figure because of the way people acted towards her and the things that happened. When she had been talking about her perfectly ordinary disposition for her own safety in the event of an emergency ("I have a little case packed with *old* clothes") there had been a rustle of incredulous amazement.

It wasn't as if she had mentioned a wig or a false nose. So there it was, a quite serious subject, but her personality had made it a joke.

And then again, the time she had interviewed a woman for a job as cleaner. "Are you a good rough cleaner?" she had asked absently. Not perhaps a usual question but a sensible one and no need to go into guffaws of laughter, although the cleaning woman was a great extrovert and given to mammoth displays of grief and mirth as if she was Mother Ireland herself.

So because she knew she was regarded as good for a laugh she occasionally put on an act and became the good joke in person.

She had kept house, had managed her life, had paid her bills, survived, but she sometimes had a very strong desire to curl up small, to sleep, to be nothing at all.

None of this had somehow touched her deeply until the strange business of Ted's *attacks*. Did you call them attacks? Or were you polite and cautious, calling them accidents? She knew a better, honester word. She knew they were irresistible to Ted. They were compulsive acts. Unconsciously by her withdrawal, her silences, her acceptances, she had been foremost in spreading this view of what had happened to Ted. They might have passed for genuine accidents but for her.

No doubt in the end Ted knew this.

By dwelling on these thoughts about Ted, she set free in her own mind impulses which would have been better curled up. Like bracken, they uncurled their fronds and hourly grew in colour and energy.

Like all people in her position she was an opportunist. When she saw something that offered the experience she desired she took it. Shallow, thoughtless, selfish, there were moods in which she seemed unable to be anything else.

Such a mood was on her now. She turned out the light, snuggled into herself, like a cat, an elderly baby, a cocoon, a mummy.

So she waited. Then she heard footsteps. They were the last thing she ever did hear.

The hospital where Joanna worked was a large teaching hospital. It was a lively crowded place swarming with young nurses, medical students and doctors. There were always a lot of romances and off-romances going on, with partings and meetings.

It was a place where things were happening, real work being done, careers going forward. In spite of being a hospital where enough people died, it was vigorous and cheerful.

There was an atmosphere of celebration in the Path. Lab. that evening. It was not strictly their party, they rarely had much to celebrate, but a party for a young man who had worked there for a spell before transferring to his real love, obstetrics. Mel Fisher had just heard that a paper of his had been accepted by an honourable society, and that not only was it to be published among their proceedings but also he was invited to read it before them at a future meeting. It was his first step forward. A great future glowed before him, he saw himself already knighted, a member of the Royal Society, a name to be written large in the history of medicine. Fisher's law, the Fisher variant, even, wonder of wonders, Fisher's disease. He was almost overcome.

The whole place buzzed with the news, they welcomed it and enjoyed it with him.

It was quite a time before Joanna was missed.

Mel was a simple boy, the son of a widowed mother. He had slaved away on the paper for twenty months now and he saw no point in hiding his pleasure.

"It's a big honour," he said solemnly to Alice. "Of course I thought they'd be interested, you know, but to ask me to read it, in person, there's a lot in that."

"Indeed there is," agreed Alice.

She poured a cup of coffee and cut the large chocolate cake loaded with walnuts and fudge that the triumphant Mel had brought in. His idea of pleasure was still a good feed, and when you came down to it, thought Alice, even the most sophisticated of them were eating their chocolate cake and drinking their coffee with extreme pleasure: Mel would go a long way.

"Have you ever read a paper?"

"I did once," said Alice with a smile, she was forty to his twenty-five, "it was at the Anglo-Chinese Convention in 1946 and it was on the chemistry of genetics, and no one understood a word. It was at the end of the War, you did things like that then, it was supposed to make people more friendly. You wouldn't even remember."

"I do *just*," said Mel.

"Funny to think I may be largely responsible for Red China," mused Alice, "with my incomprehensible little paper."

"Not largely," said Mel.

"Joke," said Alice, but she liked him. God help those mothers in labour though, their way would never be lightened by a glint of humour. Still, such solemnity allied with such good manners and skill destined him for the highest honours. No doubt

154

whatever about the knighthood, and probably a barony.

"Joanna once read a paper before a lot of French doctors at Aix-les-Bains," said Alice looking round, "but we've none of us made the Society." She looked round again. "Where is Joanna?"

"She went off," said Dr. Dick Noble, the research chief, Joanna's official boss, strolling over. "She's bound to be back, though."

"I keep getting telephone calls for her," said the Department secretary, looking harassed. "*And* for you, Mr. Fisher, *six* telegrams." She looked reproving and handed them over.

He looked at them quickly, went red and pushed them in his pocket.

His friends eyed him sympathetically. "Mum, Gran, Aunt Dora, and the twins, one each," he said.

"And the sixth?" Alice asked.

"That's from Andy, the dog," he said, going redder still.

"Doubt if my family know where I am, let alone sending a telegram," said Dick Noble. "Oh yes, they must do, come to think of it. I've been getting Charlie's letters and bills forwarded to me for some months now."

"Oh, does that mean he's coming back?" asked Alice. Dick Noble was the scion of an illustrious Anglo-Norman house whose elder brother's life was chiefly distinguished for the wide swathes of scandal that cut through it at intervals. Alice had met him once, ten years and three wives ago, and taken a great, if shocked fancy to him.

"Looks like it."

"They ought not to send him out to *govern* people," said Alice, "when he can't govern himself."

"He hasn't governed anything for the last two years," said Dick. "More like exile, poor old boy. Resident Adviser to the District Council of Mangao Mangao Federation." His brother Charles' scandals were an embarrassment to his aristocratic, even royal, relations and they had concentrated on putting the widest possible distance between them.

"I'll marry him myself one day," said Alice.

"Oh do," said Dick, "and have lots of little boys." It was strange that the blood which had produced crusaders, cardinals, statesmen, and poets, should have dwindled in the end to fat dissipated Charles and thin, academic and utterly mediocre Dick who would never have an unscholarly thought but who would never have an original one either.

"But where *is* Miss Duffy?" persevered the secretary. She was slightly afraid of Dick on account of his title, his grandeur, and his extremely short sight, which made him look vaguely and unknowingly at everyone.

"Where *is* Joanna?" asked Alice.

"*Who* keeps ringing Joanna?" asked Dick, going back, as he often did, to the point they had started from.

"Father Mahoney," said the little secretary. "He's outside now."

"Oh." Dick put his drink down. "Ah well, let me

speak to him."

Alice remembered that Father Mahoney's church was his church also. 'How they hang together,' she thought.

Dick strolled casually to the door. "He's a good chap," he said.

"Oh, of course," said Alice, irritated. She then felt ashamed of her irritation.

Dick turned round to her and smiled as if he was perfectly well aware of her irritation and even understood it.

She stood there watching for a second and wondering about Joanna. Dick was only gone a second, then he reappeared with a worried look.

"Father's pretty anxious to get hold of Joanna... something about a child."

"One of her babies, I suppose," said Alice. "I don't know. She hasn't been in here for hours."

One by one her colleagues drifted off, some home, some to more work.

"I don't know," she repeated, "she didn't say. Tell him to try the house."

"That's just it," said Dick, giving her a look. "He's been doing that. No one answers."

Joanna was still up in her sitting-room at her work table. She was staring out of the window and not really seeing anything at all.

Then she turned quickly back and sat down at her desk: she had made her resolution. It might very well be true, as she had once read, that there was a sense in which the lamb enjoyed the slaughter: but she was no lamb. She wasn't going to be slaughtered.

She locked her door and prepared to withstand the siege. If Ted came into the house she would refuse to speak. She felt instinctively that silence, withdrawal, and impersonality were her greatest protection. She was protecting herself from a ghost. Ted, as she had known him, no longer existed, perhaps, she saw now, had never existed.

She sat hunched up over her book trying to work. Viruses seemed remote and relatively unimportant. But after a bit, as she worked, taking notes and smoking, the pull of her work reasserted itself. And she became interested. Viruses have a chain reaction on certain protein molecules. This was not in itself important to what Joanna was working on; as a human reaction it interested her.

At one point the telephone rang but Joanna ignored it. It rang once some time later but still she took no notice. It was ringing outside her locked door and she did not intend to move.

As it grew darker she absently switched on the lamp on her desk without registering the progress of time. She began to get hungry but she quelled this by smoking, without really thinking about food. She had adopted the oldest protective device of all: consciously or unconsciously she was closing her mind.

Oblivious of everything except the printed page and her notes she worked on in silence. The house, the street, Oxford itself seemed strangely still with that dark stillness that comes on in some sultry summer evenings.

Outside her door Mr. Kipps called angrily to be let in: he was in the mood for company. But Joanna took no notice. She lit another cigarette and sank back into the work, only momentarily disturbed.

Down below the old grubby house creaked and stirred, the stair treads settled down, the floor boards twitched and the curtains moved in the slight draughts. Night had come and a wind was rising.

Mr. Kipps called crossly once more outside the door, a long irritable complaint. Joanna did not move.

You can dig a deep ditch for the mind but the cautious suspicious body is not convinced. She found her hand trembling and tension tightening the back of her neck. Then she realised why.

Mr. Kipps was inside when he had been out. He had crept in silently at an open front door. She knew his way of gliding silently in behind you.

She put down her work and listened. Far away down in the basement she thought she heard a door bang.

Then the telephone began to ring again.

Joanna listened: this time it did not stop. It rang and rang again. A determined attempt was being made to reach her.

And whereas once she had ignored the phone, now she longed to reach it and make contact with another mind.

But beyond the locked door was danger. Then she heard a creak of metal on metal and understood the significance of the first noise. Someone had gone out through the front door and now had closed the front gate which like many things connected with Francesca needed repair.

The house was empty again.

She unlocked her door hastily and ran down the staircase to where the telephone stood on the landing in an alcove. She turned on electric lights everywhere as she ran.

"Hello," she said breathlessly.

There was a pause, not long, but noticeable, as though the caller was surprised at getting a reply at last.

"Dr. Duffy...? Are you all right, Dr. Duffy?"

"Yes, I'm fine," said Joanna hastily, aware that she had been breathing deeply and noisily into the telephone.

Father Mahoney went on as if reassured. He sounded serious and anxious: "It's Leonie Lamond's baby. Leonie would like you to come. She thinks you could help. The child has a rising temperature and rapid breathing."

"Yes," said Joanna, trying hard to concentrate. She loved Leonie but all she could think about at the moment was Joanna... Had there perhaps been two people in the house? Could she hear the stairs move?

"Are there any other symptoms?" Joanna had

talked freely to Leonie, and she knew all about the development of the infant virus infection as traced by Joanna.

"No," said Father Mahoney. "Not yet."

"We can't be sure if it is the disease I've been working on."

"Leonie thinks so," said Father Mahoney.

"I've no cure," said Joanna sadly. "I've never done any good."

"You would be with her."

Joanna hesitated. "I've never done any good," she said again; she was so frightened of the night, the dark walk. And who would be waiting for her beneath the tree? But she did not hesitate for long, the other Joanna took over. "Yes," she said. "I'll come at once. You can say I will come."

The front door opened into blackness, the street lamp across the way was out; there was a gentle patter of hot rain on the leaves. Outside the gate stretched four hundred yards of dark street with trees and doorways from which a figure could move with outstretched hands. Beyond was the main road with lights and traffic and people.

Joanna had often said in joke that you could be murdered behind a tree in Northanger Road, Park Town, Oxford, and no one would hear, and the truth of this came home to her now bitterly.

A shadow waved in front of her and she flinched back; but it was only a tree. Something moved on her left and she jerked away to the right, but it was a gate moving.

Unsteadily she made her way towards the lights. Then she became aware of a little rustle of movement at her side, feet treading the leaves, a brush against her leg. She stood quite still, rigid and terrified.

Mr. Kipps pranced out in front of her, gay and certain of his welcome.

"Go home, cat," hissed Joanna. "Go home."

She spent a few seconds trying to send off Mr. Kipps who showed his usual density about what it didn't suit him to understand. Desperately she scooped him up, bundling him under her coat and rushed on.

Far behind her a voice sobbed: "Come back, come back." And then, as Joanna got further and further away, "I hate you. I hate you."

A few seconds later she reached the bright lights and the sense of freedom, still clutching a swearing and puzzled Mr. Kipps.

At the hospital she thrust the cat into the startled arms of the porter, who, used as he was to alarms and crises, had never nursed a cat before. "Keep him safe," she said and rushed on.

"Those medicals," he grumbled as he met Mr. Kipps' angry green gaze. "Here, nice kitty." Mr. Kipps gave him a smart box on the ears, then climbed on to the table and sat there, settling his disarranged fur and washing.

Back in the house Joanna had left, a wind blew through the kitchen window, and the red and grey dress stirred and moved, became almost alive.

Chapter 12

Miss Martin Brown

AN AGITATED WOMAN was trying to get Oxford police station. It was a measure of her upset that she tried the police: commonly she trusted her own resources. The Mental Health Visitor had lost Miss Martin Brown. She had been escorting an apparently placid, doped Miss Martin Brown from the recreational therapy clinic when her patient gave her the slip.

"Damn and blast," she muttered. "And it wasn't even my job. I was just trying to help out."

She was all the more concerned because at the therapy clinic the therapist in charge had taken her aside and asked her to watch Miss Martin Brown. "I don't like her symbolism today," she said. "She's all at sixes and sevens." They looked at Miss Brown who was arranging scissors of varying sizes in a row.

"I know they say she's non-violent. And I believe them. But look at that, I ask you. Doesn't that

164

summon up a few questions?"

On her way home Miss Brown had sat quietly by her side in the car, apparently enjoying the ride. All would have been well, and she would have had Miss Brown still demurely with her if it had not been for the tomatoes. There they were in the shop window, ripe, plump, glowing with colour, and at eight pounds for six shillings, such a bargain for bottling. "Cheap," observed Miss Brown with interest, and as her companion now thought, slyly. The Mental Health Visitor had her tomatoes, now rotting quietly in her kitchen, because like most bargains they were not so good as they appeared, and she had lost Miss Brown. "Nipped off while my back was turned," she had told herself angrily. But there it was, and the responsibility was hers; fairly and squarely it rested on her shoulders. Anxiously now she tried to pass some of it on. "Inspector? I'm glad to have got you..." But all the time she talked her thoughts were running on. Where had Miss Martin Brown got to? And even now, why?

And what the hell did the scissors mean?

Chapter 13

Joanna's Crisis

THE HOSPITAL WARD had the air of false peace, as if the whole job was over and done with, that it usually had at this time of the night. Joanna was at once quietened and stimulated by the accustomed atmosphere: this was her world. Within it she might go wrong, make mistakes, be foolish, just as in any world, any life, but they would be errors she could comprehend.

Father Mahoney was waiting outside the staff nurse's little office. The door opened as they approached and the nurse appeared. She looked frowningly at Joanna. Privately they knew each other well and were on good terms but on official occasions she was apt to be severe. Moreover, this was not Joanna's case but Dr. White's, and according to the formal rules Joanna ought not to be here at all. Except that everyone knew in moments of crisis, and this certainly was a crisis, you asked for help where help could be got. Dr.

White was of all doctors the least likely to stand on ceremony.

"I'll take you along," was all she said.

Joanna overtook her as she hurried forward and said quietly, "Can I have the case notes, chart and so on?"

"Dr. White has those, naturally; he's there now."

The implication was clear. Joanna could do no good. She agreed wholeheartedly with this diagnosis.

She noticed Father Mahoney following her.

There was a small group of people round the cot.

"She's out of the incubator?" said Joanna. She had not been prepared for this.

"Out yesterday," said the nurse absently and yet irritably. "She was making progress, you see. Nearly five pounds. Going home at the end of the week."

Leonie was standing at the head of the cot where she could see her daughter's face. She looked full at Joanna but for a moment she did not see her. Then she said, "One four eight a minute; that's pretty fast, isn't it?"

No one answered.

"Pretty fast for lungs that size and heart that size to go back and forth."

The doctor looked up. "How do you know?"

"I've been counting," said Leonie, her face distorting. "Standing here counting."

Joanna's heart was pierced at the thought of Leonie standing there counting her daughter's exhalations. And then because human nature is like that, she thought 'silly girl, does she really think she can do it accurately?'

"That doesn't mean anything very much," said the doctor reassuringly, but he caught Joanna's eye and looked away quickly. So that Leonie, if anything, was on the optimistic side.

He led Joanna towards a window where what they said could not be so easily overheard.

"What do you have on this?"

Joanna recapitulated: the virus disease she was working on had given certain indications that it entered the system through the respiratory tract, then descended to the stomach.

"Where it's a killer," said the doctor. "And it comes from outsiders, adults carrying the bug, but unaffected themselves," he went on.

He looked at Joanna with dismay, thinking that she wasn't going to be much help if she went as white as that. What he couldn't know was that Joanna was wondering desperately if it could have been she, in any way, who had brought the infection to Leonie's baby.

Joanna muttered something.

"There's very little sign, if any, of pulmonary symptoms," he went on, thinking aloud. "So it must be very early on. On the other hand, there's very little strength there."

Go on, he seemed to be saying, here's your chance. Do what you can.

Joanna took a deep breath.

"May I have the charts and the day history

please?" she said; her voice shook a little but the hand she held out was steady.

The doctor gave them to her. He was remembering strange stories about this girl. He himself hardly ever looked at any paper except for a brief look at the sports page, but he heard talk, and about this girl there had been strange talk indeed. If she was juggling with a murder as well as a sick baby then she did well to keep her hands steady.

The nurse came up. "I think it'd be as well if the mother could be persuaded to leave."

"No, let her stay," said the doctor gently.

"But she thinks the child'll stop breathing if she takes her eyes off her," said the nurse, flustered.

"Yes," he said, even more gently, "that's exactly it. Maybe she would."

He met Joanna's eyes. She heartily concurred with what he was saying, and for the first time a flicker of confidence lit up between them. He was a good doctor. They might save the baby.

"Well, I can't bear the way that priest hangs about," said the nurse, showing irritation for the first time, "as though it's dead already."

"He's come to christen her," said the doctor.

"Limbo, limbo, I don't believe in limbo," said the nurse in a hushed angry whisper.

"He helps Leonie, I think," said Joanna.

"Oh, so you know the mother? It would be much better if you didn't. Much better." She sounded distracted, moving away to the end of the room to attend to a flashing light and then back again in a series of quick movements.

Father Mahoney, who had quick ears and a well developed sense of other people's reactions, said quietly to Joanna, "I'll go if I am in the way."

"You may be," she said bluntly. "Soon, if not now, I'll tell you when."

Without noticing it she had taken charge. She very rarely came up against a real practical crisis in her work, a matter of life and death. In her heart she feared this aspect of her craft and art, which was why she had devoted herself to theory and research and pathology: the dead had no crisis in which to call upon her skill and presence of mind. She was so afraid she might fail living patients.

Now that it really came upon her she was as full of fear as she had known she would be but also full of the power to act (the nature of fear, as she saw now, was that it gave way to each little edge forward of practical action). For the moment, oddly enough, the most practical thing was to do nothing; to observe and think.

She noticed that there were still no definite respiratory symptoms. The infection was very early in its first stage then.

Observe and think.

"Very hot here," she said absently. The room was electrically heated by radiators and convectors.

The nurse watched. "I found it trying at first. Still do. Terrible on my sinus. So dry. It's the dry heat that does it."

She broke off. Joanna wasn't listening. "Did you say something about a steam-kettle?" she said in a dazed way.

"We haven't used one for nearly twenty years. I haven't seen one for over ten."

Rapidly, thinking aloud, Joanna explained the theory to her.

"A warm moist atmosphere—and perhaps the infection *cannot* get a grip in the upper respiratory tract... Hold it in check while the antibiotics take over..." but she knew, with disquiet, that the amount of antibiotics you can give an underweight baby of premature birth is small.

"There is something to be done," she said, in her mind the reading she had been doing those hours away. She had already forgotten Ted, Francesca, the house, everything. "If this is what I think then the infection is now in the nose, throat and bronchi."

"You get out now," she said to Father Mahoney. "Leonie, you can help."

A cradle was rigged up, shaded and protected with a hood, and through humid air the child was suspended in an atmosphere of minute invisible water particles. It was an improvised apparatus and it depended on faith and hope.

The child's temperature went down, the symptoms of pressure abated. Presently they saw she was relaxed in sleep.

Joanna and Father Mahoney walked home together.

"Is it a miracle?" whispered Joanna, remembering how the pressure of events had forced her that evening to read the only article that had mattered.

Father Mahoney gave a short laugh. "No. That is not a miracle. We are not metal for miracles. Just a simple suspension of the disease."

They walked on in silence for a few minutes. At the corner as they parted, he patted her hand encouragingly. "Don't think of miracles, my dear. Don't ask to be dazzled. That's not the way for you. Your way is hard work and reason."

Then he was gone.

Joanna watched for a little while, and then gave a sigh of fatigue and walked home.

'No, that wasn't a miracle,' thought Joanna. 'This is the miracle: that I am myself again.'

But the miracle was that she had been taken away from death.

Joanna walked back alone, in the early summer morning. Oxford with its towers and trees was sleeping in the pale morning light, it was very still and quiet; she felt exhausted, spent, but at peace; she was no longer afraid.

Whatever lay before, whatever threatened her she could face it. She had made her peace.

Ted was waiting for her in her sitting-room; he stood with his back to the window looking out and he turned to face her as she came in. He turned towards her with a smile.

172

Chapter 14

Coffin in Oxford

TO COFFIN OXFORD was, above and before everything else, the place where Patsy was.

But it was beginning, also, to be the home of quality murders. To him each large city had its own slight but steady characteristics in crimes of violence. Birmingham had a good line in arson; the cities of the north had a slant on breaking and entering; Glasgow specialised in family crimes with everyone called Mac-something. London, of course, had everything.

Coffin had been down to Oxford once before in the last two years in connection with a murder and found it an intriguing out-of-the-way affair with a twist in it. This case had other interests, but it was equally out of the way.

"I like a good body in a trunk," said Patsy happily.

"You've never seen one," said Coffin shortly.

"Never move house," his friend, the

distinguished and rather wicked actress, Venetia Stuart, was now recommending. "You can't think how tawdry and second-rate one's possessions look on the move."

"Not likely to get the chance," said Coffin, casting a sentimental look at his Patsy who didn't or wouldn't see.

"Tied to Mother's apron strings?" asked Venetia throatily.

"Can't get anyone to cut them for me."

But Patsy wouldn't oblige. Instead she said: "Why are you on the move, Venetia? You doing a moonlight flit again?"

Venetia's hard-upness was rivalled only and indeed caused by her monumental extravagance; three Givenchy coats and three handbags from Hermés equalled three month's starvation living in her flat. Of course when she was working such expenditure did not matter but Venetia was most apt to spend like this when she was not working because, as she sensibly pointed out, it was when you were not working that you had the time.

But apparently it wasn't so this time. "Oh no," said Venetia complacently. "I'm in the money since the *Brides* started booming, bless them. And after all I can go on playing glamorous grans for ever, can't I? No, I've bought a house."

"Actually paid for it, Vee?" said Patsy sceptically. "Cash down? Or is it a bird in the bush?"

"No, it's mine," said Venetia. Was there a shade

174

of regret in her voice? Venetia hated sitting on her capital. (Unless it was tied up in mink.) "Discovered your trunk murderer yet?" she asked Coffin.

"Probably," said Coffin. "Probably." He didn't want to discuss the case.

"Trunk cases are interesting," said Patsy, determined to be awkward. "It appeals to something deep in us."

Coffin looked displeased.

"It's the fascination of the Mistletoe Bough story, isn't it?" she appealed.

"Of course I never trusted that Mistletoe Bough story," said Venetia.

"I mean *why* get into the chest in the first place? Don't give me that line about a game. Something screwy there."

"I think you're a very clever woman," answered Coffin.

Venetia looked gratified. Patsy, he saw, did not. She scowled slightly. 'Jealous, good,' thought Coffin. He looked at her, loving her for her warmth, resilience and even for her plain cussedness: she was here and sane. She might act mad, and occasionally even in a manner to make you doubt your own sanity, but she was tough enough to hold together her own personality; she had already weathered storms that would have broken up a frailer bark. Venetia, of course, was indestructible. He had just come from reading about a woman who had not survived. The transcript handed over to him by the doctor in charge of Miss Brown was in his pocket now.

Coffin always found it easy to enter into the mind of his antagonist. It was at once his greatest strength and his greatest weakness. It meant that he could always put his hand on X or Y or Z when he wanted because he knew that X would have gone home to his wife, Y would be hiding out at a café, and Z would have fled to his Granny's lodging house in Camberwell. But to enter into the world of this person was to make contact with a curious unsteady world in which shadows, differently named, came and went; you felt sympathy, but also a measure of irritation; this woman wasn't really trying. She *liked* to be the way she was.

Coffin read:

The last time but one we met she made me cross. I walked over the road to talk to her. It was a silly thing to do. In the circumstances it was a very silly thing to do. She didn't cut any ice with me, I can tell you. I did have an ice-cream there but that was later. I am a hater, you can see it, can't you? It's always been my trouble, they've explained it to me, often and often. First I hate myself. Oh well, we won't go into that. I've every reason to hate myself. I'm bad to me. Very, very bad.

Coffin read on:

And the policeman said: Is that man bothering you and I said no bother. Do I look like a woman

*who is bothered by a man? She was, he was, she
was.*

"Yerss," said Coffin. "Very lucid."

Coffin considered all that he knew of the little
group of people concerned with the affair. They
were unknown to him personally but he had
their case histories, their pocket biographies.
While they had been weaving their lives,
agonising, puzzled, quiet men had been gathering
information.

First there was Ted, the tenant of the flat,
studio, whatever you cared to call it, in which
the trunk with the body in it had been found. It
wasn't his trunk but Mrs. Francesca Armour's
(his former landlady's) trunk, that was
established; but Ted had either borrowed it or
absent-mindedly taken it along with him when
he moved. Ted was now twenty-seven and had
been in England fifteen years. He was pretty
much anglicised except as far as his pictures were
concerned: the critics were going to go on calling
him 'fresh' and 'colonial' for years. Ted, who had
survived incredible vicissitudes—the loss of his
parents, his country, only to get good out of it
all somehow in the end as if life were continually
passing a vote of confidence in him; Ted, who
looked so dreamy and youthful but who was
almost certainly more worldly and tougher than
he looked; Ted, who had built up his own

following among critics, friends and pupils, who was a magnetic figure, feared, envied and liked; Ted was the centre of the whole problem and the most vulnerable and the most endangered of them all.

There was Francesca, Mrs. Francesca Armour; aged forty-five, educated in the Rope-Makers School, Hampstead, and Oxford; a widow since 1948, three children, all at school; a lodging-house keeper and tutor for her old college for which she taught early French philology. (She had a bad illness, this was common knowledge, in 1949, after her husband's premature death.) Francesca who was an enigma to her friends and yet not to the casual observer. Francesca who really was as open and kindly as she seemed. Francesca the missing one, but whom Coffin knew not to be missing at all, but all along in hospital, undergoing an operation for what might or might not be a fatal illness. Francesca, who had hidden herself away from all her friends like a sick animal.

There was Joanna, Ted's girl, whose work was her life. Joanna, aged twenty-five, educated at the Quaker school, Polehampton, and Oxford. Joanna, accomplished, clever, and so unworldly. Coffin had seen her father and heard of her mother. Joanna seemed a curious child for two such extroverts to conceive.

And finally, Eugene. Eugene Stanislas Czarnkowski,

said to be born in Poland—or was it Silesia? Or was it Lithuania? Education, as Sam Weller said, the world. Eugene, aged forty-five, registered alien, known to the public. Eugene, who was really no one at all.

A mannered, well-educated, sophisticated group of people with the same tastes in life: foreign holidays, opera, books, wine and good coffee. Different origins, different schools, but all arriving at the same level and heading for the same ends.

All except one. That one stood out, to Coffin, as if there had been blazing lights and waving flags. For death and violence, for the type of sexual aberration that had produced this death, there was only one possible candidate.

The motive, the clothes, the ligature round the neck, the trunk itself, all fell into place.

John Coffin from London and Pinching from Oxford got the key from the floor below and paid a visit to Gene's flat.

You could already tell that Gene would never be at home again. The rooms were still shiny, still kept in order, but imperceptibly they had taken on the character of the cleaning woman and not Gene. The chairs sat too rigidly to the table, the tables were too precisely aligned to the wall. The books on the shelves were dead, unused. The flower vases were full of early chrysanthemums, which Gene hated, the flowers of death.

Gene was gone.

Poor little murderer.

They looked quietly round, gathering up what they wanted here, what they wanted there.

"I'm taking your word on this, Coffin," said Pinching.

"You can take it."

"It fits in with the medical evidence?"

"It *is* the medical evidence."

"Otherwise," said Pinching, as if he hadn't spoken, "it's a rum do."

"Oh it's happened before," said Coffin. "Remember the case of Peter Queen and Chrissie Gall? And the woman in Westcliffe a year later? Strangled with a ligature, looked like a straightforward homicide. Only straightforward was just what it was not. Textbook stuff."

Chapter 15

Joanna is Told

MISS MARTIN BROWN, having spent the night wandering desolately round North Oxford, was glad enough to be retaken early next morning. The impetus of her hate for Joanna was gone. She no longer wished to kill her though she had been keen enough to do so last night.

Last night she had thought of herself as Jushu, the Avenger, and Joanna as the one to be punished. When she had heard of the body in the trunk she had known at once who it was and straightway dreaded that Ted and Joanna were jointly responsible. But suddenly all the feeling had drained from her. She was reconciled to herself. She was Miss Martin-Brown who called herself Rosa Mantle and who had recognised the erstwhile Miss Jeanie Low. They had been Rosa and Jeanie together in their life. Separately, she suspected, they had had as many lives as a cat, jointly they had but the one. (She was always conscious of an uncertain chameleon quality in herself and the pseudonyms were her idea.)

They had met in a hospital queue and joined forces to live in rooms in Southwark. This friendship had lasted only a short time, but it had meant a great deal to Little Brown Mouse, she had felt interest, affection and straightforward respect for her companion. And besides, she was being treated at the hospital for such a fascinating complaint. She had agoraphobia. And then they had parted over a silly quarrel about a hat. Hats *didn't* suit everyone. They had not met again until recently and then by chance.

She no longer knew whom she hated and whom she didn't; the truth is, she was muddled. Perhaps she even liked Joanna. Anyway she now wished her no harm. She had already forgotten the gas tap which she had turned on idly, maliciously, in the kitchen. She pocketed the sharp cutting out scissors with which she had planned to stab Joanna and with which she had forced the basement door of Mrs. Armour's house, and gave herself up philosophically, even willingly, to her doctors.

She took from her pocket a battered packet of Cyprus cigarettes and lit one.

Joanna looked at Ted.

And when she saw the real Ted, the false Ted,

the pseudo-Ted that her overworked imagination
had created, melted away. Here was the Ted who
painted, and got into muddles, but who was not,
and never could be a killer.

She drew a long breath. "Where have you
been?"

He didn't answer.

"Coffee?" he said, nodding his head towards
the table. It was neatly laid for breakfast for two.
"Knew where you were," he said, buttering a roll.
"Alice told me."

"Alice?" exclaimed Joanna, unable to hide her
surprise. "She knew?"

"Yes, she knew. Whole hospital knew. She was
there for a bit."

"I didn't notice," said Joanna. It was true. Alice
could have been there. She had been completely
absorbed, convinced that unless she achieved
absolute concentration the whole wobbling
machine, which included her and the baby and
Leonie, would break down and death ensue.

"You haven't been arrested?" said Joanna.
"You're not dead?"

"Not either," said Ted, pouring coffee. He
sounded grimly amused.

"One would rule the other out."

"You're not at your brightest this morning, Jo.
Did you really think I was dead?"

Joanna sat down and stared at him. Then she
touched him.

"I didn't know what to think." She added, "So

Mirry did see you?"

"She could have."

"And were you in this house last night?"

Ted looked surprised. "No, not me. I rolled in this morning."

"Someone was here. And I smelt your cigarettes."

Then she remembered the packet of cigarettes she had seen in the sitting-room of Little Brown Mouse.

"It was her. I gave her my address myself." She remembered her fears of last night. So far from disappearing they were reinforced by reason. "She doesn't like me. She meant ill. She turned the gas on in the kitchen. That was no accident."

"There's something you have to know Joanna," said Ted. "Perhaps you know it already."

There was a note in his voice that frightened her. She spoke with difficulty. "*Who* have I got to know about?"

Ted did not answer straight away, but paused as if he was seeking for words.

"Is it Francesca?"

He shook his head.

"It's not Francesca. And it's not you?"

Ted made a noise, half laugh and half sob. "Still harping on that, Joanna?"

She was not reassured.

"Who killed the woman in the trunk?"

"It was not murder, Joanna. Contrary to all the

indications. It was suicide—*felo de se*."

"But how did she get there? Who was she?"

"Gene."

"But it was a *woman*," cried Joanna. "It was a woman."

Ted said nothing, only slightly nodded his head.

"So..." Joanna shakily sat down. "I ought to have known." She thought of body measurements; the slightly curving hips, the walk—as a doctor she recognised them now, too late. "Oh, poor Gene. Poor Gene." It seemed silly to keep on saying it, but she could not stop. Then, "But I saw the *face*, and I *didn't know*."

"Because you were not expecting it... and it didn't look the same."

"No." Joanna was remembering the puffy distorted face.

"But you knew," she cried.

"I am a painter," said Ted. "And I had a special reason for having observed the features. I was painting a portrait."

"It seems too odd to think of Gene as a disorientated person," said Joanna. "When I relied on him so."

"I think there was a sort of plateau of stability that had lasted for some years. Lately it crumbled." Ted hesitated. "You remember those..." he fumbled for a word, "accidents of mine?"

"I'd hardly be likely to forget," she said.

"They *were* accidents, Joanna, I could have explained them. Only the last thing anyone wanted from me was an explanation. You were all looking for a neurosis, so you found it. I think Gene's mind became obsessed with the thought of these two incidents."

Joanna frowned.

"Think about it, Joanna. What really happened? The first time was a genuine accident, and it was due to my own clumsiness. I was working at the press in the cupboard, on students' pictures, and my tie got caught in the screw. In trying to loosen it I only tightened it."

"Like Isadora Duncan," said Joanna, half laughing.

"Well, it happened," said Ted. "I'd got it loose by the time I lost consciousness."

"Why didn't you explain better at the time?"

"Damn it, do you think I *knew* what was being said. And if I had known, you were the last person I'd mention it to." Ted was pink and embarrassed as it was.

"And the second time?" asked Joanna.

"The second time didn't exist," said Ted squarely. "The first I knew of it was when I got a touch of the gossip... that was partly the reason I cleared out. I wondered if I *was* loopy."

Joanna looked at him, not quite sure. There would always be a residue of doubt between them.

"What lay behind it? I can't think of Gene as

186

killing himself. And in such a way. Is it possible?"

"Medically and psychologically, yes. The police quoted two cases at me. People do it."

"But suicide." Joanna was desperately puzzled still.

"Suicide is a tremendous subject, Jo. People around often are shocked and surprised. But an analysis of the life of the person always turns up the evidence."

Joanna was remembering. "Gene told me a long story once, supposedly about you. But I think it was his story really he was telling me—of his life as a little boy, and when his mother died. He may have altered the details, but the basic experience was his."

"I knew it too. In that early experience, trauma, I suppose the doctors would say, everything we know about was cooked up. The masculine sub-nature because of having to be the man of the family, agoraphobia, because the experience took place in the open air, and the terrible fear of loneliness that made death look comfortable."

An uncomfortable feeling touched them that in their young, loving, but heedless life, they had somehow been selfish to Gene. But it was only a suspicion and they brushed it aside.

"Yes, suicide was built in," said Joanna. "Nothing could have stopped it happening."

They sat for a moment in silence. Then Joanna remembered.

"But why did *you* go away? Why?"

Slowly Ted drew out of his pocket a grubby, much-folded piece of paper and handed it to her. There was a famous address, a famous signature. And the burden of the short letter was a request for an interview with Ted with a view to arranging an exhibition in London for him.

"I went to London to collect all my paintings I'd left among various people, and to collect myself too," he added. "I was all at sixes and sevens."

"Oh, Ted," she hugged him. "It's the beginning."

"Not sure if it isn't the end," mumbled Ted, frightened of organised art and organised success, a stern upholder of Art versus Mammon; but he hugged Joanna back.

"The best thing in it," said Ted, "will be my portrait of Gene."

The Coroner's inquest on the body of Mr. Gene Coff, born Eugene Stanislas Czarnkowski, was held next day and a verdict of suicide was returned by a well-instructed jury. They were told of the medical evidence testifying that the strangulation was self-manipulated. Reference was made to similar cases known to the police. The lid of the trunk had been pulled down before the death rites began. It was all self-arranged, part of an apparatus of self-destroying neurosis.

There was no publicity.

So the dead woman made her last public appearance.

Francesca lay back in the high white bed and regarded them. She didn't look weak and ill, as if she had just had an operation, but cracking with energy. The nurse looked weaker.

"I'm glad to see you. I've been terribly, terribly worried about this business. I knew all about Gene. I guessed. And then..."

"You burnt the dresses," interrupted Joanna.

"I tried to burn them. I did burn some—the rest remain about in my kitchen. They seemed the essence of the whole thing to me," said Francesca. "Ted was very cross."

Ted nodded. "I thought you were off your head. Or getting at me in some obscure way."

Francesca sighed. "Poor Ted. You had troubles of your own. I didn't realise then how much I was influenced by Gene in my interpretations of these incidents." She held out her hand in apology. "You've got to realise I was sick myself. I thought I was going to die."

"You were never anywhere near dying, Mrs. Armour," said the nurse briskly.

Francesca looked at the two young people. "I thought what I had was mortal... you have to understand that. So I just went off on my own. I didn't want anyone to know... like an animal." Her eyes were bright and clear. She was a cheerful animal.

"I thought I was dying."

"You were not dying," repeated the nurse

wearily.

"Well, you have pins and needles all down your left arm and roaring headaches and spots in front of your eyes and see if *you* don't think you're dying," said Francesca tartly. "Here, give me my clothes, I'm leaving. No, don't worry, I'm a private patient, I can discharge myself."

When the exhibition was held the best picture in it was, as Ted had said, the portrait of Gene.

It was the Oxford Gene. It had all the *panache*, all the vitality and force which had struggled through so much; but the scars of the battle were there too. Ted had seen the lines left by a terrible childhood and the unending effort to move upwards from poverty and depression.

It was a wonderful portrait. It was a loving portrait.

If you have enjoyed this book you will enjoy...

WINDSOR RED
by JENNIE MELVILLE

The first of the 'Windsor' Melvilles, and never before in paperback. Charmian Daniels, on a sabbatical from the police force, is researching feminist crime and feminist criminals, inspired by her relationship with Beryl Andrea Barker ('Baby'). She takes rooms in Wellington Yard, Windsor near the pottery of Anny, a childhood friend. The rhythm of life in Wellington Yard is disturbed by the disappearance of Anny's daughter with her violent boyfriend. Dismembered limbs from an unidentified body are discovered in a rubbish sack. A child is snatched from its pram. Headless torsos are found outside Windsor.

Are these events connected? And what relationship do they have to the coterie of female criminals that Charmian is 'studying'...? All is resolved in a Grand Guignol climax that will leave the most hardened crime fiction fans gasping.

ISBN: 1 902002 01 6 Price: £4.99 Paperback

CT Publishing